WORTH THE WAIT

THE BOOK AT THE BAR SERIES
BOOK 3

KIRAHVI BELLO

OTHER TITLES BY KIRAHVI BELLO

The Book at the Bar Series

The Book at the Bar

Hooked on You

Worth the Wait

Standalones

A Chance on Christmas

WORTH THE WAIT PLAYLIST

Apple Music

Spotify

YouTube

Let's Build by Teyana Taylor ft. Quavo
In Your Eyes by Snow Aalegra
Mirror by Ne-Yo
Give Me Your Lovin by Oobie
Drive by SZA
The Story of OG by Jay-Z
Back in the A by Gunna
Welcome to Atlanta by Jermaine Dupri ft. Ludacris
Can't Go For That by 2 Chains ft. Ty Dolla $ign & Lil Duval
Type by GloRilla
Night Like This by Future & Metro Boomin
Appletree by Erykah Badu
Private Love by Sharna Bass
Thinking Bout You by Frank Ocean
Bruise by Ryan Beatty
End by Frank Ocean
Stolen Moments by Alicia Keys
Pretty Brown Eyes by JoshButlerTV
Float by Janelle Monae ft. Seun Kuti & Egypt 80'
C U Girl by Steve Lacy
Favorite Lover by Devin Tracy
New Feel by Caterra Joe
Taste by Coco Jones
The First by Young Deji

Lady Dujour by Johnny Gill
We Could Get It Together by Wee
In the Air by Destin Conrad
Sands by Dawn Richard
Straight Up by THEY.
Problems by The MSB & Chief Minosa
A Cold Sunday by Lil Yachty
Saddest Song by indys blu
Lost by N'shai Iman
Sara Smile by After 7
But You by 9th Wonder ft. Smitty
Until (Intro) by Derric Gobourne Jr
Love Song by Kirby
Sweet Lady by Tyrese
With You by Tony Terry
EA by Young Nudy ft. 21 Savage
Nine (otismadeitmix) by OTISMADEIT

BEFORE YOU READ

This book features...

* Explicit sexual scenes

* An enactment of workplace harassment

Please take care of yourself while reading.

1

GREG

I SIGNED MY FULL NAME ON ANOTHER PAGE... AND ANOTHER... AND another, Gregory E. Reynolds. Each signature got me closer to owning a four-unit duplex.

After I finished a couple of pages, I slid them to Amber with a smile. She smiled back, signing her name—Amber Cress. "I wish I was signing Amber Reynolds on these."

I tapped her engagement ring. "Pick a day and I'll meet you there. You want 200 people and the whole production and can't decide if you even want to get married in this country, in a cabin or the beach. I'm good with going to the courthouse."

She scoffed at me. "Baby, I want my white dress, and entrance, baby isle with the —."

"White roses," we said at the same time. "I know what you want. Those have been your favorite flowers forever."

Our realtor chuckled along. "Happy spouse, happy house. Glad you have a house together already." He was one of the top commercial realtors in Atlanta, and I was going to put money in another Black man's pocket. Was he also attractive? Hell yea. If he didn't have access to my social and *legitimate* wages, I would make a move on him. I've always been bi, but never publicly. I'm 6'5" and almost 300 pounds. I'm a lot of man. I've been forced to be more masculine. Nobody taught me how to express myself. I couldn't understand my own feelings. When I was fifteen years old selling drugs with friends on the block, they wanted to talk about how fine Ciara was. Not Usher.

So I swallowed my feelings and slowly began to hate who I was and what I was feeling. Until Gemini, my best friend Calvin's wife, opened the door for all three of us to experience something... beautiful. I've always been poly, even before Amber and I got together. But Calvin and Gemini are different. In a perfect world, we would all live together in a true "kitchen table" atmosphere.

Amber kept exaggeratedly signing her name again and again. "Are we almost done? I want to start my DIY list. And use my new table saw." She winked at me, knowing I bought it for her.

After everything was signed and we took pictures with our realtor at the office, I gently asked him not to post them for our privacy. He understood our...circumstance. Now we were headed to our new property. The grass needed to be cut, and the place needed a serious paint job.

But it was ours.

When we opened the door to each unit, there was an odor from being vacant for months. There was still quite a bit of work to be done. A bathtub needed to be replaced in one unit, two of the units needed new floors and cabinets, and they all needed a deep clean. Some of the repairs we could do ourselves, but Amber will need to hire and manage the contractors for the rest. She's a stay at home fiancé, so she's been looking forward to a project to dig into. I wanted this place because it's close to downtown. Midtown may be the prettier side, but that wasn't a priority for me. While corporations are buying every sliver of green space, I wanted property I could pass down to my future children. Something to outlive me. Amber wants to wait a few years until we grow our family, and I would never rush her. I own two garages and co-own Grant Library with Calvin and Ms. Grant. Now another building has Gregory Reynolds' name. Ms. Grant taught me how important it was to own property, and it didn't fall on deaf ears.

After we took more pictures on my phone in the best looking unit, the realtor left, and we stood in silence to take it all in. "I guess we're landlords now."

I kissed her forehead. "Yes, we will be. Want to grab some food?"

She leaned her head on my chest. "Duh, I'm feeling hibachi."

Perfect. The wait would be about twenty minutes, and it'll take fifteen to get there and back. Plenty of time for Calvin and Gemini to come and set up the surprise. Yea, I planned a little something for my baby girl. They're coming to do a real quick clean of the floor and bathroom. They'll set the ambience by putting out some of Amber's favorite candles. An air mattress will be by the window with fresh white sheets and white roses on the ground. My girl talked me into making this investment for us, so I'm investing in her and what she wants.

I just hope she likes it.

While she walked to the car, I bent down to "tie my shoe" and placed the key under the third rock to the left of the door. I stood up and texted Calvin where he could find it. We met up yesterday to discuss everything he would need.

"Bae, why are we back here? I thought we were headed home."

I parked in the space closest to the door. "I think I left something. It won't take long, baby. Come in with me?"

She shrugged and got out of the car. The plan is working.

We made it to unit A.

"We left a light on?" she questioned, grabbing her key. "Fuck, the bill is gonna be high."

When she turned the key to open the door, Calvin and Gemini screamed, "Congratulations!!!" while holding up a sign that read "Amber's Place."

Gemini waved the sign and danced like a cheerleader, while Calvin swayed his hips, holding a bottle of Amber's favorite wine. Mmm, tonight is for bae, but fuck Calvin's ass was cute as fuck. We need to link up again so I can lick it. We haven't had *special* time in a while. Gemini was always down to watch and participate but Amber hasn't yet. I hope one day she will so we can be a true quad.

"Ahhh y'all! Turn up!" Amber jumped up and down with them, then turned toward me. "You did this, didn't you? You know I hate surprises, but you did this. Come here!"

She jumped and I caught her with my arms around her back, enveloping her in a deep kiss.

"Annnd we will take our exit. Y'all enjoy! Congrats again!" Gemini said, pushing Calvin out the door.

When we heard the door close, she wrapped her legs around me, petting the back of my neck. Now she got me bricked up. Still kissing and licking her mouth, I moved to the air mattress and laid her down, hiking up her dress.

I was about to pull her thong down when she grabbed my hand to stop me. "Pull it to the side. I can't wait."

Anything my baby wanted. My pants weren't even off yet. I undid my button, adjusted my briefs to expose my length and slid inside. When she moaned as I entered, I was ready to cum. She was so tight and creamy. I gave her slow strokes as her hands caressed my chest, watching her face twist with pleasure, her lips puckering before she bit them. Fuck, I was so close already.

I gave her the deepest thrust as she screamed her encouragement, "Yes, Gregory. I want every drop. Finish baby, finish."

My spine shivered as my body went limp. I turned to the side and exhaled. "I'm sorry baby, you were too damn tight."

She stuck her tongue out. "I know. You like it when I clench?"

I responded with a groan, still thankful for the day we met. When Amber handed me my bottle at Green Envy Gentleman's Club, I fell in love. Her face, her body in the all black jumpsuit. I needed a ring on her finger pronto.

"You remember when we first met?" I asked, pouring her glass as we sat on the air mattress.

"Mmm hm, talking about 'excuse me miss, can you help me find your new last name?' Then my dumb ass was looking around because I thought you said napkin."

I kissed her cheek. "Now look. Our second property together is a duplex. You know I'm naming this after you, right?"

Her face scrunched as she looked at me. "After me? Why?"

"Because you're my wife." I said confidently, pouring my glass. I'm speaking our union into existence, no matter how long I have to wait. "Of course this place will have your name on it."

She raised her glass. "To the Reynolds Family."

"To our family."

I raised my glass in agreement. I can't wait for our family to grow, through birth or adoption. When we're ready, we will have our family.

We clinked glasses.

WHEN WE FINISHED OUR FOOD AND THE BOTTLE OF WINE, WE fucked all over that unit. Against the refrigerator in the kitchen, the air mattress again, in front of the sink in the bathroom. By the time we exhausted ourselves, it was two o'clock in the morning. After we appropriately christened everything, we cleaned up, packed the car, turned off the lights, and went back home.

I hope one day someone has as much fun as we did.

2

GREG

I was headed to The Reading Room, a coffee shop in Decatur, for a date with a fine ass woman I met at the gym a few weeks ago. After exchanging numbers, we started feeling each other. I told her I was engaged and in a quad. She was hesitant after I let her know what that meant. It took a FaceTime call from Amber saying they were engaged and that she had her own girlfriends to enjoy for her to believe me. They were talking for so long, I knew if I let it continue she would steal her. My girl is such a flirt. After their conversation, "Gym Baddie" was down. I sent her name, age and picture to Amber before I started driving to the coffee shop we were supposed to meet at. After driving for two minutes, future wifey was calling.

"She fine! You sure you don't want to share her?"

I shrugged to myself even though she couldn't see. "Gotta ask her."

"How you pull that?"

"How did I pull you, wifey?"

She did her corny chortle. "Boy stop, you installed the security cameras at the new place?"

"Yea, and added the uh motion detectors around the

outside. It's already connected to your iPad. It took a minute, but I wasn't paying anybody to plug in that stuff wrong."

"Bet! Have a good date! Make her cum for me! Also send pics of her pussy and a video of you eating it if she lets you."

I growled, "You know it baby. You have fun tonight too. You cleaned your strap?"

"Hell yea, always. I stay ready. Because when you stay ready…"

"You don't have to get ready I know. That's why I keep rubbers in the car and my wallet."

"Yea it's still Atlanta and we don't do raw with no tests around here boo." We laughed. "I love you, baby. Your location is locked in."

"Yours too, babe. I love you too. Be safe. See you when you get home, whoever gets there first."

"Bet." I blew a kiss and hung up the phone. I parked down the street and was about to get out of the car when I looked at myself in the car mirror. "I look good as hell." I ran my hand through my beard with a nod.

As I walked away from the car, a thick shortie with caramel skin and brunette bob waved as she was leaving the coffee shop.

"Hey boo," she said with lust-filled eyes. "Thanks for picking me up from here. Want to go to my hotel?"

"I thought we would talk and chill for a minute. But that's fine, just text me the address." A charming smile graced my face. I opened the car door for her, and she slid in the passenger seat.

After she texted the address, I sent it to Amber and put it in my Maps and headed there. Bae and I always shared our location, but any address changes got sent beforehand so there weren't any surprises. No cap, I was ready to dig into her guts. Her ass looked natural and good as fuck on the StairMaster. The only kind of body I like.

We wasted no time after passing the threshold. After the door closed, she already had her shirt off. Her lime-green bralette was holding her double Ds back, her nipples showing her excitement. She pulled me onto the bed. I bit my top lip as she wrapped her legs around my hips, kissing my neck, playing with my beard. "Do you mind if I kiss you?" she said in panting breaths.

I hummed, hovering my lips right above hers. I slowly licked her bottom lip as she groaned, opening her mouth for me. I had one hand on her thigh, squeezing the juiciness while she kissed my shoulders and ears. I lifted her face and deepened the kiss, brushing my tongue against hers, her heart beating faster. When her hand brushed across my nipple, I rubbed my dick on her seam. "Once the beast is awake, you can't run."

She brushed her hand down my chest, undid my button and lowered the zipper. My dick fell out on full erection. "I'm not a runner." She massaged me from base to tip with a gentle squeeze. I leaked with precum that she played with using her thumb.

"Mmm, keep doing that," I groaned. I lifted my hips to start pumping her hand. I wasn't afraid to make noise when it felt good. She slowed down her speed, lowering her body to the floor, putting me in her mouth. "Damn."

She scooted off the bed to her knees. I barely had time to push my pants all the way down so she could keep going.

"Can I put my hand on your head?"

She nodded with her mouth full as I put my hand behind the back of her head. She went into overdrive, started to deep throat then pulled me out, sucking on the balls. She'd been waiting to taste this dick.

"Shit, fuck," I moaned with the stroke. Her lips were covered in Fenty. Now the Hot Chocholit Heat was smeared and it made her look even sexier. Then her thumb started to rub circles on the top of my thigh. I needed to take back control. I pulled away, taking a few steps back.

"Did I do something you didn't like?" She asked.

"Hell nah, it's my turn to make you wet."

She slowly stood up. "Mmm, it started feeling too good?"

I licked my lips. "How about I show you how it felt?"

She smiled, floating back onto the bed. "How about you show me then." She took off her leggings and lightly dropped them on the floor. "You do the rest."

I leaned on the bed with my forearms, pulling her panties off, kissing the dark spots on her inner thighs, the moles next to her lips. Then traced my tongue on her sweet wet gap. She tried to move her hips to ride, but I held her down. I lifted my head to meet her eyes. "You told me to do the rest, right?"

She groaned, "Well do it faster! Fuck the head."

I scoffed with a devilish grin. "You deserve what I'm about to give you." I sat up, grabbed my pants and pulled out the gold wrapper. Once the condom was on, I was back on the bed, my beard just above her expectant face.

She leaned up and kissed me as I slid inside. "Mmm," we sighed together. I started with a slow hip roll to find her best spot. Her hands rested on my broad back. Her nails brushed my sides and ribs. I thrust deeper, her scream confirmed her appreciation. I leaned back and lifted her legs so they would rest on my chest. "Fuck Greg, yes yesss." I kept my tempo watching her make different faces. *My favorite part.* Her eyes were squeezed shut as curses tumbled off her lips. Her pussy pulsed on me. "Cum on that shit."

She whimpered as I flipped her around and gave her the hardest back shots, sweat flying off of my chest and neck. She had a flower tattoo right at the base of her spine. I brushed my thumb on the stem, and she shivered as another rush came like a faucet at full blast. I stroked again against the wave as her moan hit another octave. I was starting to rise too.

I quickly pulled out and turned on my side as I came with a scrunched face. After a few deep breaths, I stood up, went to the bathroom, and flushed the condom down the hotel toilet. Then I grabbed towels, one for me and one for her. I laid the towel across her, but she still didn't move.

"Make a noise so I know you're alive."

She groaned, "I'm up, I'm alive." She slowly rolled and looked up. "I haven't squirted in months."

"I bet." I walked back into the bathroom and turned the water on.

"Ooo, do you want to take a shower together?"

I shook my head. "That's only for wifey. If I didn't have to meet up with somebody, I wouldn't be leaving so early. You gonna be here later?"

She nodded her head. "You know I'll stay up for you."

I nodded then showered and put my clothes back on. As I was drying my beard, she asked, "Where are you going anyway?"

"Nowhere."

"Well have fun if I don't see you tonight."

"See you later."

When I got back in the car, Amber was the first one on my mind. I called but it rang and went to voicemail. She was probably still working the threesome she planned with her favorite girls. They weren't best friends, but had play dates, if you catch what I'm saying. My trap phone was off the hook with four missed calls and six texts. Looks like I'm the delivery man tonight.

> Wifey: Headed to do some orders on the East Side

I drove from Decatur, to Stone Mountain to Conyers. Amber texted to ask me to pick up the latest Kennedy Ryan release from Eagle Eye Bookstore. I was telling them Amber Cress, but she made it under Amber Reynolds. I smiled when they handed me the bag. I love how that sounds. While driving home, I realized she still avoided conversations about setting a date like a plague.

I pulled up in our driveway and parked next to Amber. I didn't want to see my car again tonight. I figured she would be done by the time I made it back to the West Side. I walked through the front door, turning off the outside light. I know she's not mad at me when she leaves the light on. I know after she showered and washed her hair she was out. I love the smell of her hair because it smells like sweet potato. She was going to be mad when she had to deal with her hair in the morning. But now, I can't wait to see how beautiful she looks in bed.

I've known Amber as the rough and kind woman, my little Libra baby with a Leo man. She calls herself bi, but I haven't seen her with a man besides me in a long time. When we started talking, I asked if she was open to the poly lifestyle. Imagine my surprise when she told me about her membership to an invite-only swingers' club and was down. When we went together, she introduced me to her girlfriends. They look amazing together. It was nice not having to explain what terms meant. She understood me and where I was coming from, more than anyone else I'd met at that time. She's shown time and time again why she wears my ring on her finger, my *engagement* ring.

I quietly took off my shoes and moved through the silent, dark house. When we were house shopping, I told her that she could pick everything and design it. Just no pink. I really just wanted to watch her smile through the process. She connected with an interior designer that followed the perfect vibe. She calls it "Afro Janpandi." We have some good art pieces and warm colors painted on the walls with round furniture. It's clean and minimalist. As long as our house brought peace and a smile to her face, I knew my world would keep spinning. All I cared about was having a safe and secure place with a door and windows to lay my head. Amber fills my lungs every time she's close to me.

I slowly opened our bedroom door and peeked inside. Her arm was lying off the side of the bed. Her teal bonnet shined in the night. When I walked closer, her breast was hanging out of her tank top. I wouldn't want another woman in her spot. She's set the bar so high and changed my life. Amber is going to be my wife, and I love her for saying yes.

I showered again, since I sweated in the car, dried off and put on my gym shorts. It was going to be warm anyway, Amber had two security blankets. One was a crochet blanket no bigger than five feet by five feet that was a gift from her mom, the woman who abandoned her. Then me. As soon as I laid my head on the pillow, her hand sleepily tapped me. "Mmm, bae."

I scooted closer to her, wrapped my arm around her, and kissed her shoulder. "It's me, baby. Good night. I love you."

"I love you too, night," she whispered, falling back to sleep, snuggled against my chest. She may think of me as her shield, but she's really mine. She's seen me on my good and bad days. I need her forever.

I just happened to also like watching her eat another girl out.

You know what? That's what I'm going to dream about. Damn, I didn't ask gym girl for a video. *Oh well.*

3

GREG

I was getting started early today. A quick pop up to a shop, drop off some orders, then swing by Coraline's lounge. It's dark now, and it'll probably be dark again when I come back. Amber was still sleep when I got up from the bed, so I got ready in another room.

Dressed in my Dickies with a change of clothes in a bag just in case, I opened the fridge to grab my drink and it had a note.

Check the microwave :- *

I opened the microwave door, in it was my lunchbox, still hot and packed with another note on top.

I hope this meal is as hot as you.

A.Reynolds

. . .

I'M ABOUT TO WAKE THIS WOMAN UP AND GIVE HER SOME BACK shots, then drag her to the courthouse. The last name on here needs to be made true. Yea, I'm using the hard points on her ass the next time I'm digging her out. I bit my lip thinking about the face she made the last time her ankles were tied. I tucked the note in my pocket. I had a special place for them in my drawer. I grabbed a breakfast sandwich out of the freezer and a bottle of water for a quick breakfast before heading out.

I pulled into Reynolds' Repair Shop on Bankhead playing Jay-Z. This was one of the two locations I owned. The other on Cleveland. Bull, the inspirational business man that introduced me to drug dealing, taught me a lot. But I'm not on the same path. Instead of giving kids cocaine to push, I created a scholarship program to set them up for success. If kids didn't want to go to college, then I tell them to learn a trade and investment. I've been to every high school in the county to talk about the automotive industry. I pay for five students to go through a technical training program to have a guaranteed job at my shop. The requirements to apply to the program were to have their high school diploma or GED, read three assigned books and write a 500-word essay on why they are interested and summarize what they learned from the books. I usually accepted everyone that applied.

My night job was kept under wraps.

I always kept my two worlds separate. Reynolds' employees never touched the drugs and the drugs never went through the door. Well, at least the front door. The general manager, Mr. Demonte, knew what happened in the background and was a quiet backup man.

I was always intentional with keeping the staff safe. What they didn't know wouldn't hurt them. But every few months when I needed a large shipment, I'd arrange through Coraline, CEO of Grant Enterprises and Calvin's older sister.

I dabbed up Monte, the fifty-year-old previous garage owner. He wore black Dickies instead of the uniform blue. Since he was so close to retirement, he asked to work for me part time instead of becoming a voting or library volunteer, and I agreed. He did just enough to stay busy, but not overbearing. His wrinkled eyes and salt and pepper afro would always be welcomed here. I trusted his judgment to keep everything together while I moved around. I never have the availability to be here all day everyday so he gives me trustful updates. "Morning, Monte."

"Good morning, Son. Didn't know you would see us today. I thought you'd be in Midtown."

I shook my head. "Nah, I was there a few days ago and everything was straight." I went into my office and he followed. "How we look today?"

Monte looked at his clipboard and flipped a couple pages. "Good, couple of oil changes, brakes and a tire change. I placed an order for some tires, they should get here tomorrow. And Luke is doing some overtime Thursday and Friday. He said he talked to you."

"Yea I approved."

"Cool. Also, uh." He wiped his nose. "One of the new kids keeps messing with Terry. She said she's fine but something's off. Those jits know better than to mess with her."

My ears perked at the mention of Terry. Not only was she the youngest on the crew at 21, she was one of three women on our team. "Who's been fucking with her?"

"Tron."

Fucking Antron. He said he would be better if I gave him a chance. His essay wasn't the greatest, but I knew he was twenty-three with a seven- and three-year-old.

I need to hear Terry's side of the story and document each

step so Antron couldn't come back and sue me for wrongful termination. I just hope she tells me everything that happened because I need to get to the bottom of this. "Ask Terry to come in here."

Monte stepped out and let Terry in. She had chestnut skin and had her knotless braids in a low ponytail, wearing a red bandanna. She was wearing the uniform, navy blue Dickies short-sleeve coveralls with her name stitched on her chest.

"Have a seat."

"I tied up my braids, Boss. Mr. Monte already talked to me about how waist-length braids are dangerous, so I tucked them away. See?"

"No, this isn't about that." I leaned forward and folded my hands together on my desk. "Can you tell me about how Antron was treating you?"

She rolled her eyes, her bottom lip twitching. "I mean, he's not the nicest guy here. But I know how to handle him."

I blinked. "You're working, you shouldn't have to handle anybody. Even outside of work. Has he done anything inappropriate?"

She looked away and balled her hands together. "I don't want him to get in trouble."

I knew Terry was thankful for the job. She wrote 1,000 words with her application two years ago when she graduated from South Atlanta High School. Some program graduates moved, or worked with other shops. But Terry enjoyed coming in. I just need her to speak up right now.

"I want you to be able to come here and be comfortable. We go way back and you're an amazing employee. Please tell me what happened."

She sighed. "He got my number from my file and... sent me a dick pic. He stares at me all the time. I know I'm the only girl on our shift, but Tron is the only one that pushes up on me. I've been here for a while with no problems. Niggas will speak, but nothing inappropriate. It's just him. But you know." She sucked her teeth, leaning back in her chair.

I clenched my teeth behind my lips, trying to swallow my anger. How did I let this slide for so long and not notice? "Thank you for letting me know. I'm sorry this happened. He shouldn't have went in your file and stolen your personal information. We will handle this." I paused and looked away from her. "Do you have any other disturbing messages from him?"

She took out her phone, opened her messages and slid the phone to me. I picked it up to see multiple messages from the same number with no response. I recognized the number as Tron's cell.

You look good mama. Let me lick you up bitch. Come to the break room I'll give you some dessert. Picture. Picture. I'm in the bathroom thinking of you baby, I'm spraying this on your back.

I wanted to throw her phone against the wall from the messages. In my shop? In the shit I own? Hell no. "This is completely unacceptable, T. Antron shouldn't be harassing you like this. You don't have to worry about this anymore."

She nodded. "I blocked him. I can send you the screenshots."

"Thank you. Can you please write down a summary of everything to give to Mr. Monte? Please let us know if you need anything, additional support. Anything."

Terry got up from the chair. "Thanks, boss. You know, I've really enjoyed working here. I never saw myself as a corporate type. I like working with the cars. I hope to open a garage too one day."

I smiled, standing up to shake her hand. "You can do it. I believe in you. I'm glad to be the stepping stone to get you there. We can have additional time to sit down and talk about a business plan, how much it'll take, investors and everything. Let me know when you ready."

She smiled wider. "Thank you. I'll get the summary to

Monte before I leave," she said as she walked out of my office. I was happy she had a plan outside of this shop. My dream is really helping people know what they want and don't want in life. How dare Tron's stupid ass try to fuck with her without her consent? In my shit? In the building I worked for and bought? Fuck that.

When Monte came back in he knew the look on my face. "We need to post a position, don't we, Son?"

I grabbed a pencil from the cup on my desk and snapped it in half between my fingers, my fists still shaking.

"I'll take that as a yes. These young boys don't know nothing about respect or how to keep a job. Always trying to chase the cat at the wrong time."

"Antron needs to bring his ass in here, now." My veins filled with ice. I wanted to put my hands on him for doing that dumb shit.

Monte nodded and walked to the garage. I watched through the two-way mirror as he got Tron from under a car and brought him back to the office. Tron walked in with a smug grin as I stood to my full height and build.

"So you like fucking with Terry? You blowing up her phone with shit, at work."

Antron rocked side to side, scratching his chin. "Shit, she like me like that, Boss? I'm still talking her up. I know she wanna fuck a real nigga."

I slowly walked around my desk. "What?"

He sucked his teeth. "It aint that serious man. I know she want me. She put that makeup on for me, doin her hair all cute and shit with the lip gloss. Girls don't wear a beat face to work on cars. I needed the digits, so I pulled it from her file while Monte was out one day."

I got in Tron's face, towering over him. I had at least 150 pounds on him. He was ninety pounds soaking wet. I sneered and looked him in the eye. "I need your badge now, and your uniforms dropped off here, tomorrow morning. You're fired. I thought you were better than this. I took a chance on you, that you wasted." I wanted to say I'd snap his neck in half if he crossed the threshold of the front door again. But I've seen enough courtrooms to last me a lifetime.

Tron twisted his lips and shoved the card in my hand.

"Get off my property," I growled.

He sucked his teeth again and walked out of the garage, cursing and tapping his foot on chairs. I turned and saw Terry sigh a breath of relief.

"Let me change my clothes so I can help with a couple things. I've got some time."

"Yea we need it," Monte said, heading back to his office chair.

"Oh, so you're not helping old man?"

Monte groaned as he sat back down in the office chair. "Well somebody gotta answer the phone, Son."

I laughed as I grabbed my Dickies to change into.

After knocking out the oil changes and tire rotations, and smoothing the wait time over with the customers, I went by the house to shower and change again. I'm a big ass man, and I always need to smell good. I don't step out if I'm not at my best. I combed and oiled my beard, then brushed my hair for a wave check, rubbed lotion on my arms and chest, put on dress pants, a polo and dress shoes, checked the mirror with a sexy smile, then took a couple photos. *Nothing wrong with admiring what looks good.*

GREG

I PULLED INTO THE VALET IN FRONT OF CREAM'S CIGAR LOUNGE. "Good evening, Greg." The short attendant with a platinum bob said with a wink.

I winked back. "Wassup Tracy. How are you tonight?"

She eyed me like she'd dive in the car so we could fog up my windows. "Oh I'm good. I get off at midnight, any plans?"

"I'm busy, but text me later."

She tried to contain her excitement. "Oh definitely. Coraline said she was expecting you. She's in her office."

I looked down and inspected my attire, navy blue dress pants with a gray polo with matching J's. *I look straight.* I walked into the smoke-filled air. My clothes won't stink because of the air filter system Coraline has throughout the place. The dark walls brought a calming ambience where men and women could feel good and smoke what they wanted. Glorilla was playing as conversations flowed around the room, dancing like the smoke in the air as I made my way toward the back.

I went up the two flights of stairs and turned left where I was met with her security lead. I dapped him up and he moved to the side to let me in the corridor. There were three black doors and a bookshelf. I approached the bookshelf and pulled *Coraline* by Neil Gaiman, the latch and the bookshelf swung inside of another room.

The room had mirrors and gold wallpaper. I approached the second mirror, slid it to the side and typed in the four-digit code. After a ding, the wall and floor slowly turned, exposing Coraline's office. Her office at Grant Enterprises had glass walls with views of downtown. She used this office to show her true self.

The walls were painted an earthy green, and the dark hardwood floors were complemented with leather furniture and a sixty-inch TV. Across the room was her large black desk with three monitors, one being multiple camera POVs at the corporate building and downstairs. She sat in front of a wall with floral paintings. The way the petals fell and opened, they were definitely vulvas. I always knew Coraline was a lesbian. I never saw her stand next to a man and be happy. She had a certain taste, and her taste was Angel at Green Envy Gentleman's Club. Everyone knew she was a weekly visitor and nobody could check them or their "special" relationship. A dancer fucking the CEO isn't a new concept. Even though I heard Angel was married, but that was none of my business. I just would never date one of my employees.

I only met Coraline here when discussing certain business since I shouldn't be seen around the corporate office for a million and one reasons. She had wiped her hands of the drug business when she sent peace offerings to her rivals after her mom, Ms. Grant, retired. Everything had been calm since, or so she thought. When Ayden got ran up on with Casey in the house, Coraline found out too late to smooth it over before Bull, Casey's dad, stepped in to "fix" it.

It only made the problem worse. Coraline had no choice but to send Casey, Calvin and Gemini to New York for a weekend for their safety. She met with a rival with me by her side as protection. Now, here we are, still silent partners as she now has to get back into the "dirty" side. She arranges and buys the tree from trusted associates. I sell and bring her the money, with a fee. She benefits from the extra money on the side and we trust each other to be discreet.

"Wassup CEO boss lady," I said bopping into the room.

She rolled her eyes, wearing her black suit and white button-down with the top buttons undone. "Don't 'wassup CEO' me." A small smile grew as she stepped away from her chair toward the seating area. "Niggas got too hype in Houston, costing me $50,000 in damages. Now I gotta find a new manager. Then, a magazine reaches out to me for an interview. What the fuck am I supposed to say?"

"Maybe, 'Hi I'm Coraline, CEO of a national entertainment industry before 35?'"

Her eye twitched. "You can't sum up my job in a sentence like that. I'm not doing it. The reason that people get killed is because they're easy to find. I don't want people to think they know me or can find me. I have to protect my family. I'm supposed to keep everyone safe. Now, I'm back on the drug shit, so I'm moving quiet and in the background." She rubbed her temples. "Anyway, how's business on your end?"

"Which one?"

"The legal one."

I rubbed my beard. "I had to fire a cat today. I wanted to hem him up, but I can't do that as a manager. So, I let him go."

She shrugged. "It happens. That's why most people that work for me are contractors. They can come in and out as they please, and HHH takes care of the actual validity of their shit for as much money as I pay them. Helping Human Helpers is the most expensive but thorough hiring company." She sighed, taking a sip of her soda, "How's fiancée doing?"

I sucked my teeth. "Still aint decided a date. I was ready to settle down years ago."

Coraline laughed and patted me on the shoulder. "Settle? You've fucked my brother, my sister AND my sister-in-law." She exaggeratedly turned her head to the side, causing her shoulder-length silk press to bounce.

I laughed and hated that she phrased it like that. "First off, it was consensual. Those also are multiple relationships that can't be summed up in a sentence like that."

"Are you not concerned with your behavior?"

I fake gasped. "My behavior, C?"

She made a face that reminded me of Calvin. Those two could go back and forth all day, but in the end, they cared for each other a lot. I'm glad I don't have any siblings.

"I've never pushed up on you though."

"I been knew you've had a crush on Calvin and just fucked Casey cause she wouldn't give up on you. Now Gemini? Surprised me. But hey." She put her hands up, "I ain't judging."

"Well I guess I'm lucky you're not attracted to me."

She gave me another look. "And be the final Grant on your roster. I don't fucking think so. Money is the only thing on my mind."

"I know someone else on your mind too." I made another face at her.

"Shut the fuck up. Are you rolling or not? Coming in here fucking with me. I shouldn't have given you the code."

"The code? You mean *The Kingsman* and *Spy Kids* process to get to your office? You change it every few months anyway."

"Nigga just roll the damn blunt."

I laughed louder and opened the secret drawer in the coffee table and took out the grinder and rolling tray. She lit her cigar carefully, then stood up. Since her office was on an upper floor, from below it looked like a black ceiling. For her, however she could see everything. Coraline always wanted to see all and know all at all times. I thought I was bad, but I don't know how she sleeps at night. A CEO doesn't need to be in the business this deep. But it was started by her mom. I can't even remember how old she was when she started working for her.

I finished rolling and began smoking the blunt, standing by her observing the bar and couple dozen people smoking cigars too. She ashed her cigar. "I have a question, but don't judge me."

Her lips twisted. "What?"

"Why haven't you told your siblings about this place? I can tell you like it and keep it safe."

"Because here I can... be me. I watch the cameras, meet with security. I hired everyone here. If my siblings found out, they would want to hang out here or know where to find me. Next thing I know, ops would be here. As long as they think I'm the professional, mean CEO sister, it keeps them safe from here."

"Safe? Like this is a bunker?" I asked.

"Nah, I've got different coordinates for my bunker."

I broke my neck looking at her. "Coordinates? Damn that's a lot. Amber and I can come through when the world ends? I can read a map."

"See here niggas go. Already inviting themselves. I've seen that *Twilight Zone* episode when everyone breaks into that man's house to get to his bunker. Calvin can read a map and it's him, Gemini, and Mama. Casey and probably Denver. With you and your bae, me included that's nine people."

I counted on my fingers. "Nine?"

We both ashed in the tray. "Someone else would be there too. That's none of your concern."

I nodded. "You want a hit?" She shook her head no. "Why don't you smoke tree? I've seen you go through gars." All the times I've smoked with her, she always declined a hit and would take out a Black & Mild or premium cigar.

"Tobacco is guaranteed to kill me one day. I'd prefer to keep cashing death."

"Do you want to talk about it?"

She blew smoke out her lips. "Nope."

For a few silent moments, we just people watched. When I was tired of standing, I went back to the couch. "I'm assuming another shipment is coming."

She nodded. "Right. Tomorrow night, at ten o'clock."

"Bet, I'll be there. Everything will be taken care of."

———

I STOOD IN THE LOT WITH MY HANDS IN MY POCKETS. AFTER A few minutes passed, three Nissans pulled in, parking close to where I was standing. Marcus got out of the car first. We communicated through Coraline to help keep things under wraps. We never wanted digital communication to cross us.

"What up Greg." We dapped each other up.

"Wassup bro, whatchu got for me?"

He nodded his head toward the trunk. "Big C said she wanted the premium loud shit. My connect hooked us up real good."

I eyed the other cars. It was usually just us when we met.

"They're straight cuz, you don't need to tense up."

My eyes met his, then I patted my waist while walking to the back of Marcus's car. "I'd hope not nigga."

He opened the trunk door. There were twenty large vacuum-sealed bags of product in the truck. *That's weird as fuck.* It looked fresh and didn't have a scent, but wasn't even tucked away in a suitcase like it didn't need to be hidden while they drove. *Noted, don't react.*

"Imma head to my car."

I walked back to my car and grabbed the duffel bag that was placed in my backseat while I was at the lounge. Coraline knew better than me to walk in with the bag, so she had security place it in the car for me.

I leaned back out of the car and found five men looking back at me with crossed arms. Fuck. "Yo what's going on Marcus?"

"We have a message for Big C. If she wants to keep us as partners, she needs to pay more money, bitch ass nigga."

I sucked my teeth. I knew this was going to be bullshit. "She ain't tell me all that. Is the deal good or nah?"

"Nah bro."

I threw the bag back in my car, walked to the driver's side without turning my back to them and sped out. I didn't even care they were still standing there. I wasn't about to get robbed. I called Coraline when I was blocks away.

"How'd it go?" she asked. I heard pots and pans clanging in the back. She must be cooking.

I sighed loudly, still driving with no destination, checking my rearview mirror anxiously. "I need to pull up. It didn't go."

A pot slammed, echoing in the background. "Shit shit don't come here. Meet me at the park on John Lewis. How far are you from there?"

I typed it in my Maps. "Fifteen minutes."

"Alright I'm twenty away, leaving now. FUCK!"

Then the line ended.

I've only seen Coraline really angry at certain times, and she becomes a different person. The anger of a Virgo is scary. She'll break something, or drop it, then have a calming professional spirit overtake her. She fixes whatever is going on quickly and quietly. The fact Marcus made a scene in front of strangers was even worse.

I knew I shouldn't have gotten out of the car when the other cars pulled up. What if they were cops? I thought we were being careful enough, but Marcus has been infiltrated. I can't tell Coraline that over the phone. So I got to the park as fast as I could.

I beat her there and parked in the shadow by a streetlight

that shined yellow like a golden flickering cover. I was tapping my foot against the pedal, scratching my beard, looking at the time. Marcus fucked us over.

Coraline's Mercedes pulled in and parked next to me, the lot was empty. I got out of my car with the duffel bag and sat in her front seat.

"I need you to tell me every single thing that happened because Marcus's bitch ass is pissing me off."

I told her everything from where we were standing, the people that were out of the cars looking back at me, and what Marcus said word for word.

"More money? We shook on Five G's two months ago, and that's what we've been doing. Did he even say how much more?"

"He said he would take it up with you."

Her phone rang with Marcus's name. She waited a few seconds then answered. "So you mad?"

I heard him mumbling but couldn't hear what he said.

"Honestly, fuck all that. I'm not saying another word to you man. Lose my number and stay out my clubs, fucking punk baby ass bitch."

Then she ended the call. We sat in the car in silence other than the buzzing of the light above us. "I'll try to get ahead of this to find a backup plug. In the meantime, use your stash. I'll hit you up when I can get more."

I handed her the bag and she threw it in the backseat. Then blew out air.

"You couldn't have planned for this C, it's not on you."

"Well it doesn't feel like it."

I nodded. "Drive safe. Good night."

"Night Greg."

I got out of her car and quickly into mine. Before my door was even closed, she was out of the lot. This was going to bite both of us in the ass, I knew it. I'm not going to tell Amber yet. I made it home before midnight since they were doing middle of the night work on 285. I showered and put on briefs and got in bed with my future wife. I held her close and she sleepily scooted closer to me.

I can't imagine my life without her. Tonight could've gone much worse... I was lucky.

5
___

AMBER

I woke up and stretched. Greg was out of the bed already, so he was gone for the day. I rubbed my blanket from my child-hood. The colors were faded, the edges frayed, and there were multiple tears, but it was all I had left from that part of my life. When I was three years old, my parents left me in the house alone for two days. A neighbor did a welfare check and saw me in the kitchen eating jelly from a jar. Child Protective Services tried locating my mom and dad but they just, evaporated into thin air.

So, my neighbor took me in and raised me instead of me being surrendered to CPS. Mrs. Fezra and her daughter, Liya, were the closest thing I had to a family. They were the reason I even graduated high school, let alone college. How they reached out and cared for me, even when my attitude was sour, inspired me to be a school counselor so I could pass knowledge and encouragement to the next generations. When I graduated with my bachelor's in psychology, I could tell Mrs. Fezra lost some weight, but I was so happy she was there that I ignored it. Then when I was away at an internship in Tampa, Florida, Liya called me in tears and said she passed away in her sleep. She had cancer, but didn't want chemo. She didn't want me to be off focus. I was grieving so bad that I lost the internship due to "poor performance." The funeral was in California and I didn't have the money to go to the service.

I still see her face sometimes, or she visits me in my dreams and asks how I'm doing. She had jet black hair and always wore black eyeliner, even as she continued to age. Whenever she wanted to help but didn't have words, she would pat my hand and squeeze. Every time. She'd be able to tell me how to get married. She was married, and divorced, three times. She would say "Amber, whicha head thinkin' self, that boy loves you, so love him back, you hear?"

I laughed as a tear escaped from my eye. "It's been so many years, but feels so fresh," I said out loud to myself. I texted Greg good morning and got my day started, took a shower, brushed my teeth, did skincare, detangled my boho knotless braids and oiled my scalp. *I'm not a little girl anymore.*

After staring at my drawer for minutes, trying to decide on the set color of the day, gray seemed best. The matching sports bra and legging set with a pullover looked cute as I threw a deuces at the bathroom mirror. My purse was packed with my wallet, keys and snacks. I was planning on getting to Pilates early so I could be close to the front. I'm so thankful to have found this studio. It's Black-woman owned and only fifteen minutes away, a true blessing in Atlanta.

When I got in my BMW, Erykah Badu started blasting from the speaker and I nodded along, putting my shades on. Even though it was cold, the sun was still out.

I placed my water bottle in front of my claimed machine and did some side stretches, trying to mentally prepare for class. I felt a tap on my shoulder and turned around. I knew the girl's face from being around the studio but, I didn't know her name. Her locs were styled into a high ponytail, and she had a worried look on her face.

"Hey, psst."

"What's up?"

She pulled me to the side and whispered in my ear, "You have a hole in your leggings right above your... you know."

I gasped and sped walked out to the bathroom. She followed with her bag. I bent over the mirror and saw the growing hole right on top of my crotch. If she hadn't brought it up, I probably wouldn't have noticed until my legs were spread eagle. My spot was right in the front of the class, and that would've been too embarrassing, especially if the hole got too big.

"Thank you so much girlie for letting me know. My coochie was about to be on display for free. I'm just going to take my water bottle and just head back home for the rest of the day. That was way too humiliating."

"No, please don't leave yet. I've got a pair of shorts in my bag that I keep just in case, and I think they're your size. Just wear these."

She dug into her black gym bag. *Literally Black* was stitched on the side with Black Authors Matter on the bottom.

"That's a cute bag," I told her.

A huge smile filled her face. "Thank you girl!"

She handed me the black spandex shorts, and I put them on in a restroom stall. They fit me perfectly. I walked back out and exhaled as I admired myself in the mirror. "Thank you so much. I can't tell you how much I appreciate this. What's your name again?"

"You're welcome! It's Che'Naomi, but call me OG. I'm glad that it was before class got started too, because I would have held up a towel to make sure people didn't see your... sacred place."

We laughed and walked back to our spots. Before class got full, OG moved to the machine next to mine.

Today's session was painful, but I was definitely seeing my

muscle definition more. As I was packing up, OG asked if I wanted to go to a coffee shop close by, and I surprised myself by saying yes. She seemed cool and was a "girl's girl" so why not? It was a short walk up the street.

Since it was my first time here, I may have spent ten minutes looking at the menu. Reading every option over and over to decide what was right for me. Can you tell it's hard for me to make a choice? "Have you been here before?" I asked her.

"I have! Their grilled cheese croissants are really good."

I nodded, scrolling through the ingredients. "I don't know if you can tell, but I like to process all of my choices." I chuckled to myself. "Now that I've marinated the options fifty times, I'll have that and an iced coffee."

"Awesome! It's on me."

I shook my head. "Please, you saved me with these shorts. I'll pay."

The man behind the corner looked to each of us. "I just need someone's card."

I handed mine to him before she could reach in her bag. He gave us a number, and we sat at a table. It's been a while since I hung out with a "friend" and not one of my girlfriends. I hope I don't come off too awkward.

"So what do you do?" OG asked, sipping a glass of water.

"Well I'm technically a stay at home fiancée until I decide the wedding date. But I'm working on a duplex and overseeing the construction and all that. You could call me a project manager."

"Ooo! Congrats on your engagement! I'm a visual artist, bookish content creator, business owner," she said, patting her bag. "If you need books, bookmarks, kindle inserts to book covers, I got you!"

I nodded. "Very bookish. I love that! I need to read more."

OG's smile grew. "If you need some recommendations, I got you. But they will only be Black authors."

I took out my phone. "I am all ears."

OG gave me ten books with their tropes. I screenshotted every book cover, seeing how fast I could get them delivered.

When our food came, we asked each other random questions, exchanged numbers and social media handles. We only sat for an hour, but the time flew faster than I realized. It was nice to know that strangers still look out for people. We hugged as we left. Since I got her website and was mass ordering books anyway, I got some bookmarks from her website too.

As I walked back to my car, I wondered if Greg was having fun at the library deep clean. I hope he and Calvin get good personal time together.

I know he misses him.

6

GREG

I PULLED INTO THE LIBRARY PARKING LOT. CALVIN AND A FEW overtime volunteers came in every other month to help deep clean the library. I signed up since I haven't seen my man, I mean my friend, in a minute.

Calvin stood in front of everyone, putting his gloves on. "Thanks for coming for the deep clean. We have a checklist, so put your initials next to the task." The list included a variety of tasks like window washing, desk deep clean, vacuuming elevator tracks, dusting ceiling fans and bookshelves, and more. Everyone initialed, grabbed supplies, and began cleaning.

I was able to focus for thirty minutes until I noticed Calvin was bent over vacuuming the elevator tracks. I pressed my lips together and focused on wiping down the desks. *Fuck, his ass looks so good.* I couldn't help but be reminded of the feel and taste. We've been working our way up to penetration, but shit his head game and touch is enough for me. Then the faces he makes while I jack him. My knee started bouncing. *Calm down.* I've had a crush on him for so long that I don't know when I didn't. I could never pick one gender for life. That's why I'm thankful Amber understands how I see myself. Not many women, I've met, are into the poly lifestyle.

But if I had to leave the world and pick between Calvin or Amber to escape with, I'd choose Amber every time. But nobody better fuck with either of them. If it wasn't for Gemini, I never would've had the courage to be a part of that beautiful threesome.

I stopped dusting the bookshelves and walked over to him. We were on the second floor so everyone was under us working with headphones on. He had some on too. I brushed my hand against his back and he jumped. "G! You fucking scared me."

"Let's go in the closet," I said, maintaining his eye contact.

His jaw dropped as he looked up at me. "Everyone is working. Like how *we* are supposed to be."

I eyed his growing bulge as he looked up at me, a familiar position between us. "Someone wants you to come with me. Nobody has even come up here to look in a minute." I nudged my head towards the janitor's closet.

He bit his bottom lip, moving his supplies out of the elevator. "You know I can't say no when you're looking down at me." He grabbed everything quicker and moved it to the side, grabbing my hand and pulling me into the closet.

In the dark, with the smell of lemon and vinegar, our bodies pressed together. I rubbed my dick against him as he hummed. I bent down and kissed him as his arms wrapped around my waist. He snuck his hand up my back and I groaned. I brushed my hand on the front of his jeans, wanting to feel his excitement.

As we made out, I undid his pants, easing my hand past his briefs. Calvin groaned too loud and I placed my finger on his lips. "You gotta be quiet, baby."

I slowly stroked him as we continued to kiss. I started easing onto my knees...

"Calvin! You up here!"

We quickly pulled away from each other as Calvin tried to zip his pants before shuffling out of the closet, hiding his bulge. "Hey! What's up?"

The door closed as I sighed. We were so close. When I heard them get farther away, I walked out of the closet with a bucket as a cover. Nobody was there to see it, but I hope it made a difference. After a few minutes, Calvin came back as I was wiping down the back of a chair. "That was close." He chuckled.

I made a face and chuckled back. "Shit what do you mean? If we had more space, I've would've had you sitting on my face. What are you doing after this?"

"Nothing. What do you want to do?" He looked at me over his glasses, which made me want to bite his lip.

"Get a drink and see where it goes," I said with a wink. Then my phone rang with "Future Wifey." "One second." I stepped away to answer.

"Hey baby, what's up?"

"I'll be with my girlfriend Mimi for a couple hours at her place. I'm headed there now. As a little update, the new appliances for unit B got delivered and installed yesterday. Everything has been painted in unit C, but they fucked up and got the paint on the good floors. So I cursed the manager out. He's fixing them for free."

My girl always meant business. That's what makes her a great manager. "Good girl, my baby, you deserve a treat. After she's done with you, you'll be mine when you're ready."

She giggled. "Yes, daddy, see you later on tonight. Any plans?"

"Calvin is coming over." I looked at him, looking at me. "We'll be in the guestroom."

"That's fine, I don't care. You know I can sleep through anything. Tell him I said hey. Love you."

"Love you." The line ended, and I walked over to Calvin

wiping the windows. "I'm free tonight if you are. Then maybe you can come by the crib."

He smiled so big. "Good, let's hit the bar then."

Everyone cleaned for two more hours then were dismissed. Calvin quickly locked the doors as I watched him walk back to the car. I got in mine and followed him to the bar closest to the library. Ironically, the same place I told him to go over a year ago where he met his now wife, Gemini. They were dating, engaged, and married in under two years. Meanwhile, Amber can barely decide how to wear her hair, let alone a wedding date.

I'm not okay with waiting longer to be married. Our five-year dating anniversary is coming up in April. I'm tired of saying my fiancée. What if something happened to me? Nobody would be able to make a life-changing decision for me. My family is gone. All I have is her and Calvin, they mean the most to me.

"Somethin' is on your mind," Calvin said to me, sitting down at a table. "Wassup? I see you thinking hard."

"Man I'm just ready to get married. There's niggas avoiding a ring like a plague, but I'm ready for mine. I already bought the ring I want her to wear for the rest of her life, or until it's upgraded in ten or fifteen years. What if something crazy happens to me? A hospital won't listen to her if I was in a coma, but they would if she was my wife. There is a legal support you have being officially married to somebody, not just roommates. I would be down for a domestic partnership with anyone besides her. She's my wife, point blank. Not a nesting partner. Maybe it's not that serious with her?"

Calvin put his drink down and looked at me. "You can't think like that. You know Amber loves you. She's just... maybe taking her time to think about it. Try to talk about it again with her and see? If she wants something big, you'd have to wait awhile anyway."

I rubbed my forehead. "Nobody is trying to wait that long, man. It pisses me the fuck off. Why doesn't she want to be with me? If she doesn't want to be poly anymore, I'd close everything off. I really would."

Pain showed in Calvin's eyes.

"I didn't mean..."

He shook his head. "Don't worry about it. That's your woman. I would respect that, hands down. Gem and I only do stuff with you, so with us it's like a Vee relationship, with me as the hinge. She's been okay with us doing stuff solo and joining, but she doesn't have a girl... I know she really wants to. Maybe if her and Amber hung out more, it would help. We've only been married almost a year, and I get where you're coming from. Wedding planning is a bitch. Gem yelled at me for wanting a gentleman's cake. Like a cake? Really? I wanted a mini library in there, but we weren't about to lug 100 books for the guests."

That made me chuckle and take another burning sip.

"Anyways, y'all still have to talk about it. I know you're busy running around the city doing what you do, but you need to make time for her too. Dedicated time. To have a heart to heart conversation. You have to make sure you reconnect with her."

I nodded. "Would you and Gemini want to come over next week? Movie night? No expectations, just chillin' on the couch, match a couple of blunts."

He dapped me up. "You know we can come through."

I texted Amber to see if she was free next Saturday for a movie night. After she let me know she didn't have anything planned, she put it into her calendar so we could stock up on snacks.

"I know I need to reconnect with Amber, but I want more time with you."

He looked surprised, then eyed me up and down. "You do?

Well we do need to finish our conversation from earlier. Is Amber home?"

I shook my head. "Not until later."

Calvin stood up. "Then it sounds like we have somewhere else we need to be."

I took my wallet out my pocket. "I got the check. Don't worry about it." I went to the bar and gave the money to Al, the bartender.

"The rest is your tip, man."

He nodded, "Ight. Have a good night man. I'll need something off you too."

I tipped my head. "I'm busy tonight. But text me tomorrow."

Al acknowledged me and typed on the POS machine. "Ready?" Calvin asked.

"Hell yea." I would grab his hand, but I don't like to do stuff in public. I'm not ready yet.

I beat Calvin to the crib. As he was walking up to the door, he was on the phone smiling. It had to be Gemini. I could hear her voice yapping on the other end.

"I'm glad the dinner I made was good baby. I just pulled up to Greg's house... Gemini says hi... and hopes that we go all the way."

My eyes widened. I didn't even know what to say because the thought of seeing Calvin's legs in the air made my body hot. The faces he would make, how tight he would be. *Fuck.* I'm so ready to dig into him, my man.

"Bye baby." Calvin hung up the phone. "I'm sorry I wanted to talk to you about it first. But, I did want to try... you know."

I gently grabbed his hand. "You don't have to apologize. I've been thinking about it too and didn't want to push it. It seems like we've enjoyed any other time we've been together."

He blushed looking away. "Yea we have. Gemini has been

fingering me too." His eyes began to roll as he exhaled then looked me in the eye. "I want you. I can handle you now, all of you."

I began walking to the stairs, with his hand in mine. "Why wait? We can get started now, it's just us in here."

He followed me, not letting my hand go. We went into the guest room. I closed the door as he took his shirt off. I hummed. "You really think you're ready for all of me?"

He quickly took off his pants. Then placed his glasses, wedding ring and phone on the nightstand before getting in the bed. "Didn't I say that? Now take your clothes off and come here. Relax."

I took a deep breath, took off my wifebeater and briefs, getting into the bed. Feeling Calvin's skin against mine helped calm me down. I wasn't sure what to do. Suddenly, being close to him made me feel vulnerable. Sometimes I craved it, right now it felt like a spotlight was put on me.

"Greg, get out of your head. If you don't want to, it's okay." He laid his head on my chest.

He reads me like a book. "No that's not it," I replied. "I want to, really bad. I just don't want to hurt you."

Calvin kissed the center of my chest. Then the base of my neck, slowly kissing me up to my ear. "You won't. We have lube in the nightstand right?"

I nodded. "I haven't moved it."

I exhaled and closed my eyes as he kissed under my beard. "Okay then. I'm right here with you. We'll listen to each other, like how we always do." We kissed as I brought my hands up his back, pulling him on top of me. My hands flowing from the sides of his waist, down to his ass.

"I'm here with you." We continued to kiss until he trailed kisses down my arm, then my stomach to my dick. As he slurped me, I held his head and started stroking his face. Calvin hummed, sending shivers up my back.

"Damn baby, suck your shit."

He sped up causing my hips to flex. He was really doing his big one as I laid my head back. He snuck a hand under me and squeezed my ass. I surprisingly growled. "Fuck."

He squeezed my ass again and slowly sucked my tip. I rolled him on his back. I was on top of him. Looking down trying to hold in my growl as he met my eyes. I kissed his chest, down to his hip, licking his dick and slowly bringing his legs up. When my tongue graced his hole, he groaned loudly, holding my head. Then I stroked him with my tongue as his knees shook, swirling in circles.

"Fuck, that feels so good," he moaned. "Baby don't stop."

I licked his gap. "I wasn't planning on it." Then I entered the tip of my finger inside. He's so tight, shit. His knees twitched as I started to tease him. In.. and out. In...out...lick

"Dammnnn." Calvin said easing himself more and more onto my finger. "You're filling me up already."

I kissed his thigh, up to his dick and started slowly sucking, pushing in the rest of my finger as he whimpered for more above me.

"You want another finger?" I asked.

"Yes, yes give it to me," he groaned with his hand on my head.

I slowly pulled out with my middle and index finger crossed, Calvin gripped the sheets. I moved slow so he could get used to it. But hearing his moans made my dick leak with precum.

"That's right, stretch that shit for me. You look so good. Take it. Take that shit."

After he could take both fingers, I continued to stroke, watching his face, his legs shake. Damn he was so fine.

"I want that dick," Calvin groaned. "I'm ready."

"Are you sure you're ready to try this?" I asked. "I have no issue waiting longer."

"Yess," Calvin whimpered . "I want to feel connected to you in all the ways that's possible. You mean so much to me. Let's go there together."

My dick jumped.

"You know I can never tell you no." I reached over into the drawer and pulled out the lube, slicking it over my dick. I sat it at the front of his entrance, swirling it in a circle before I slowly pushed deeper. He was so fucking tight that it made my shoulders shudder. Then he moaned under me, his bottom lip quivering.

"Deeper... deeper," he whispered.

I slowly pushed in deeper, filling him in all in places of pleasure. "You're taking it so good. Damnit." I started slowly stroking him. Fuck how did this feel so good! The deeper I went, the louder he moaned. A shiver of pleasure crossed by body. I loved it. I loved it so much it was making my knees weak. Then when I looked in his eyes and saw how he looked up at me. *Damn.* I could spend forever with this man. Calvin started rubbing my chest and lightly squeezed my nipples, causing a growl to escape my throat. I didn't want to pound, but these slow strokes were doing something to my heart.

"You feel so good," he whispered. "Don't stop keep going. I'm yours."

Mmm. "I know it baby." I pulled all the way back and pushed all my dick inside as he gasped.

"Greg," he said with a gasp. "You're fucking the shit out of me."

"Mmm you said it's mine right? And I'm yours. I want you to feel all of me." I slowly rolled my hips against him and he dug his nails into me. I lightly lifted up his legs as he screamed yesss. Damn I can't hold it.

"I love you," he groaned. "I love you so much."

Hearing his voice say it was like a gentle kiss on my ear. "I love you too Calvin. I'd do anything for you."

"Nothing can break us apart. I'm with you. I got you, forever."

I moaned so loud and gave another strong thrust. "I'll always have your back. Fuck, I'd do anything for you. Where do you want it?" I growled above him.

"I want it all inside me." He brushed his hand across my chest and my dick twitched as I came. A guttural noise came out of me as I finished. This release was different, it was like I'd been holding it for years. I can't describe the feeling of watching him be pleased. Seeing him happy, made me happy. I slowly stroked him one more time, getting everything out like he asked. Then I rolled to the side and caught up on my breathing.

"Fucking shit, Calvin. You got a nigga trippin. That felt too good."

He brushed his hand up my back and my shoulder. "I've been tripping over you. That felt amazing."

"You took all of me. I wasn't expecting that. I didn't know what to expect. Everything flowed so easily."

Calvin sighed. "I told you I would. You were worried for no reason, now come here." He reached out his arms for me.

"Shit, let me grab a towel for us first." I stood up with a groan and went to the closet for them. I wet both of them and wiped ourselves clean. Then I got back in bed and held him. Feeling his head on my chest, my hand brushed his back. There was so much about Calvin that I loved. I couldn't even start to list them. I've always felt like I could be myself around him. He's never judged me. If anything, he's always understood where I stand on us.

Even thinking about the bar last night, when I mentioned maybe closing off relationships, he looked shocked but understood. Amber is my future wife. Well my wife if you ask me. Calvin is my best friend, my partner. We've known each other since high school and have just reached the place where we can be ourselves, share ourselves.

I love him. I love Amber. I love Gemini.

We are a unit. A family.

I didn't think I could be this happy.

Then I drifted off to sleep.

7

———

GREG

I LOVED WAKING UP WITH CALVIN IN MY ARMS, BRUSHING MY thumb along his spine. I kissed his forehead as he moved in the sheets. "Good morning," he said, nuzzling closer to me, his nose tickling my chest hair.

"Good morning handsome." I kissed the top of his head, my arm wrapped around him.

"What time is it?" he said, tracing my sternum.

I reached for my phone and checked. "It's 7:30. What time do you need to leave?"

"Close to 8. I need to shower, but I don't want to leave your arms."

He squeezed me tight as I pulled him closer. I hate when he left. He's only a call away but still. Maybe one day we could all live together, but that would be a dream. I brushed my hand up his back. "If you keep touching me like this I won't let you leave until 10." We laughed as he got out of the bed with a grunt.

After Calvin showered and got dressed in the same clothes he came in, I walked him to the door, holding his hand. "I really had a good night with you," I said.

He kissed the top of my hand. "Me too, thank you for being

you." We stood in front of the door. I looked at him, he looked up at me, licking his bottom lip. I lightly kissed his lips, then his mouth opened and we leaned into each other. My hand brushed his ear as I held the side of his face. His hand rubbed my lower back before pulling me in more. I rested my forehead on his. "I'll miss you."

"I'll miss you too," he whispered against my lips before kissing me one last time. Then he opened the front door as I held it for him, getting a last look of his gorgeous ass as he left.

"Text me when you make it home."

He held up his phone. "I will. See you later."

After I ate an apple in the kitchen, I heard the saw in the backyard. I know my babygirl is working early in the morning. She got in late last night from Mimi's. I saw her on the cameras. When she came into the house, she didn't knock on the guest room door or anything. Just went into our room and closed the door. The guest rooms were way down the hallway, so she couldn't see or hear us.

I walked under the porch and waved at her. She waved at me and turned off the saw, lifting up her glasses. "Hey! I'm just building the supports for the cabinets. We are not paying people for the stuff we can do."

"Mmm, lookin' all sexy moving that saw."

She posed with the peace sign. "Thank you baby, how's Calvin?"

"He's good. We actually went all the way last night."

Her jaw dropped as she yanked her safety glasses off. "Oh I need to hear about this." She moved around the table and came to me. "How did it feel? When did you start? Were you nervous? Did he do anything to you? Tell me, tell me."

I chuckled bashfully, looking away. "Wifey, all these questions."

She lifted her arms and placed them on my shoulders.

"That's a big step. Like, that's your first time with a man like that. I'm proud of you."

I held her waist. "Thank you. I was nervous because I never... I never knew him and I could feel closer than we already did." My heart was beating fast. I could still hear him moaning like he was right next to me, feel his clutch on my dick. "It was amazing. I uh... I loved it. It felt like we were making love. Well, we did make love."

She smiled at me. "I'm so glad. You all have come a long way. I didn't want to bother, but I do want to watch you two together. When you're ready."

I quickly nodded. "I'm not yet, but I will be one day." I brushed the sides of her body and pulled her back into me. "Now, I want to reconnect with you. I'm taking today off from everything. I have a project idea I need your help with."

Her eyebrows raised. "Really? Let's hear it."

"From watching the people walk on the sidewalk, I didn't know it was that busy. What if we built a little walk-up library? Get some free books in the neighborhood or some coloring books for the jits."

A large smile grew on her face. "That is perfect! When did you want to start?"

I shrugged. "Today? Tomorrow? Monte can run things without me for a few days. I don't need to run orders or anything until later."

She jumped up and down. "Oooo, my baby is gonna be homeeee to do a project with meee. Yes!" She skipped away from me and went back inside singing. "The cabinets can wait, let's research!"

We immediately started watching videos in the living room. Amber was notating the measurements and pieces while I was figuring out the cost. We aren't broke, but hell we need to budget to not blow everything. I've got fifteen bands on the side right now for our honeymoon. I'm not telling her when we go.

I'm not even telling her where we're going. I'm packing her bag, and we're going to the airport. It's taken her years to decide a wedding date, she won't be planning the honeymoon to be two years out.

We bought the wood, paint, stain, hinges, and the piece of glass so people can peek in. I tried to use the drill, but Amber stopped me. She was quick and in her element. Her being confident in this project made her not only attractive, but it brought me peace. I remember when she was working two jobs as a school counselor and bottle girl at Green Envy. She was barely sleeping, couldn't keep food down and her hair was falling out in clumps. I told her to quit both and gave her double what they paid her in two weeks.

Now, she was doing what she was passionate about, and I was the one helping her.

I love this woman wearing these wood-safe glasses and cargo pants, like she's a Black *Kim Possible*. We actually had real conversations, the new pose she mastered in Pilates class, the car wash I've been spitballing to raise money for the Auto Mechanic Pathway Scholarship. It was like when we first met and could talk all day every day.

"I'm surprised that only took us a couple hours to do," I said stretching. Even though I was a little tired, Amber had a smile the entire time and talked like she wasn't being timed. I enjoyed listening. She even suggested a mural of Maya Angelou on one side and LeVar Burton on the other. I liked the idea, and she started searching for artists.

After we showered and laid out on the couch, I asked her, "Anything else you want to try?"

A devilish grin crossed her face and she looked at me. "What if we did a theme night?"

"A theme night."

"Yes! We can role-play. Maybe a cowboy and city girl run into each other." She brushed her index finger across my chest. "If you want to have a little... fun. You're not too tired from today right?"

"Fuck no, it's been a while since we role-played. I will buy a pair of Levi's and ten-gallon hat right nah." I stood up. "You mind if I leave and come back dressed?"

She licked her lips. "I don't mind, Mr. Cowboy sir."

I was actually excited to role-play with just Amber and me tonight. It's been a while since we tried this. I went by the mall, driving way faster than the speed limit, came home and changed clothes in the garage: black Levi's, a leather belt, and a cowboy hat. A nigga doesn't need a six-pack to be sexy so I aint wearing a shirt.

I walked into the kitchen, and out came my baby in a thin, neon yellow short dress with large gaps on the side that showed her bouquet of roses tattooed on her left side. I eyed her sexy body in the dress that stopped a centimeter past her pussy. *Her ass is mine when she turns around.*

"Oh! I thought I was the only one in this Airbnb."

Oh yea, the role-play. I pulled the piece of hay out of my pocket and put it between my lips. "I was here alone, miss lady." My drawl was horrible and she was trying to hide her laugh. "I got here first, ma'am. If you want to sleep in the bedroom, you'll have to fuck for it."

She eyed me up and down, slowly walking toward me. I noticed she was wearing her red bottoms and it made my dick throb more. She pulled the hay from my lips. "Well I guess I should start now," she said, rubbing her hand on my bulge. "I don't have anywhere else to go. I'd be a good fuck for you."

She bent down like she was about to suck me, instead she yanked my belt buckle with her teeth and stood back upright, turning around slow so her ass brushed me. I guided my hands down her thighs, blessing each mark. Feeling her skin was addicting, I couldn't get enough of it. She knew I'd fold with her standing in front of me. I could tear this dress to pieces right now and spread her open, heels in the air and all. But I want to take my time.

I traced my hands up to her waist, then up her spine as she rolled her ass against me, moaning. "Where could a gentleman like myself," –my hand clutching her neck, then down to her breast –"fuck you mercilessly." I began playing with her nipples.

She whimpered, standing up closer to me, bringing her neck toward me to kiss. "Anywhere." She sighed.

I turned her to face me, then bent down, picking her up and placing her on the bar stool. I got on my knees in front of her beautiful glistening pussy. My dick throbbing to feel her walls. My mouth watering to taste her.

"Mmm fuck." I didn't even move the dress as I dove in. As my arms were holding her steady on the chair, my tongue made her squirm. Stroking her, rubbing my nose on her clit. I smacked her ass and felt the plug. *Oh she wants to take all this tonight.*

I slowly stood up as she adjusted her seat on the bench. I started pulling off my belt maintaining Amber's eye. When both ends of the belt were in my hand, I smacked it to the side with a *THWHACK.*

Her legs crossed in the seat as she eyed my chest. "Kind cowboy sir, I was fucked by your tongue. Can you fuck me with something else?"

I traced my index finger against her vulva. "Do you think you've earned it babygirl?" I only put the tip of my finger in as she started to beg.

"I've been good, don't I look good sir?"

I pushed my finger slower and deeper inside. "You look damn good. Good enough to eat and keep eating." I slowly pulled my finger out. "Come over to this couch, you've got more tongue fucking to take. Sit on this face."

Running on her tiptoes, she came to the couch. Instead of strangling her legs around my waist, they were around my shoulders. Her ass was in the air as I brought her even closer to my mouth, licking her to base and back, playing with her plug, slowly pulling it out and putting it deeper. Each time I turned and stroked, she groaned louder and louder as her arms and head were rested on my thighs. Her arms were shaking and she convulsed so hard that I held her tighter so she wouldn't fall forward.

She was taking deep breaths as she slid back down. "Fuck, I knew that would be a good position." Her knees were still shaking as I scooped her up in my arms, carrying her up the stairs, biting her neck every few steps, kissing and licking between others. I threw her sexy ass on the bed and she was face down, ass up on her hands and knees. The bedazzled butt plug even gleamed in anticipation.

I squeezed her love handles, massaging her thick ass, pressing two fingers in her velvet slickness. When I did the "come hither," the "yes yes yessss" tumbled out of her lips.

I slowly pulled out the plug. "You want more, baby? Tell me what you want."

"Your fist. I want the whole hand, daddy."

I added a third finger and with a twist and turn, I added a fourth. She stretched and took it all up to my knuckles. Before tucking in my thumb, I licked her clit. When she couldn't take anymore, I slowly pulled my hand out, putting the juices on my dick before putting it in her ass.

Goosebumps rose on my back as I started to slowly stroke, seeing her wear the plug was so sexy. I reached for the lube on the nightstand before going deeper. After pouring that on, she screamed, clutching the sheets.

"What's our word baby?" I asked to remind her.

"Sour," she groaned, slowly pushing her ass against me.

I grabbed her wrist and pulled them to her back and went faster, pounding and squeezing her wrist tight. "Just like that," she egged. "Fuck me, I want my dick. Who's pussy is this?"

I rolled my hips, digging deeper into her as she screamed, "Mine. This is my shit right here, all mine."

"Yesssah," she panted as I went faster and faster, pressing her wrists into her back. I smacked her ass hard and she yelped. "Harder!"

I reached my hand back and smacked her other cheek harder, my hand stinging. I released her wrists, caressing her back, kissing up her spine. My sweat pooled on her skin as she grinded back into me.

"I love you," she whimpered.

"I love you too, Amber." I leaned forward kissing her shoulder. "You're perfect, you're the woman of my dreams. I've never met anyone like you and never will. I can't wait to be your husband."

Her walls tightened against my dick. "Say it again."

"I can't wait to be your husband," I said into her ear. I tucked her braids to the other side of her. "You're the love of my life. I can't wait to be your husband."

She turned around, wrapping her legs around me, easing me back inside. "I want to be your wife. baby. I really do."

I looked down at her in the eyes. "Are you sure baby? I can't lose you."

She started winding her hips against me, stroking me from below. "I'm sure. I love you too much to let you go." She leaned up and kissed me, her tongue dancing in my mouth. We flowed for so long in the bed, that we stood up and fucked against the bed frame. We couldn't keep our hands off each other. When we finally got exhausted, we threw ourselves on the bed, still holding hands.

"So you were on demon time with the plug."

She shrugged, getting up from the bed. "I wanted to surprise you. I also liked getting more time with you today."

"I liked it too. I love seeing you in your element and happy. We have date night coming up too. I hope you still like me then."

She chuckled. "I'd still go even if we were mad. We'll just be mad in the car and fix our faces when we get there."

8

____

GREG

I came home early, got out of my work clothes and showered. Calvin texted this morning confirming the linkup. I was excited to see them again.

Amber was adjusting her leggings. "I don't know why I'm nervous. It's only Gemini's first time here, right?"

I came and rubbed her back. "Baby you don't need to be. She's cool and open. We maybe exactly what both of them are looking for. But no rush. If you're uncomfortable at any point tonight, I won't push it no more. You have my word."

She nodded to herself and adjusted the placement of the snack bowls again.

They walked through the door five minutes later, matching in all black. Gemini in a black short set with Calvin in a black t-shirt and shorts. Everyone hugged and made their way to the couch. "I love the colors y'all used in here Greg, it feels warm," Gemini said, admiring the entryway décor. "I like the lamp in that corner. Did you hire someone? This looks really professional."

"It was all Amber," I said smiling at her.

Gemini turned and looked at Amber who was trying to look

shy. "This is cute girl! I thought I was the only one with the good eye," she said with a wink.

Calvin and Gemini sat on the couch, getting deeper under the blanket as Amber brought everyone's drinks. "Gem what do you do for work?" she asked.

"HR supervisor with Helping Human Helpers or HHH, whatever you want to call it."

"Ohhh I read an article the other day about the AI platform y'all were launching to answer questions. Since it's 24/7, it'll save costs or something?"

Gem rubbed her temple. "It's been a headache because some people love it, others hate it because of how AI has ruined the water supply in cities across the country. I'm on the implementation team, so the rest is confidential. I signed an NDA, so I legally can't say more."

"Damn that lock and key?" I asked.

"That's what I said," Calvin added, sitting to Gemini's right. "They've been having my wife work Saturday mornings with no extra pay and denying her PTO time too."

"At least I'm remote and it's only a few hours," she said with a shrug.

Wife. It made me jealous to hear Calvin say it so effortlessly. But I have to keep waiting. I sat down on the other side of Calvin. "Now don't drink too fast. Remember that last time that happened."

He eyed me and sucked his teeth. "I had five shots and a margarita at that bar crawl. You would pass out too. That's why I won't go ham like that again."

"I wouldn't pass out, but I'd definitely be drunk as fuck not walking straight. I liked carrying you anyway." I shoved my shoulder with his.

Amber chimed in, "How about we do a lift challenge to see who can pick up the most people in the room?" She stood up flexing. She was more toned, but Pilates can't be that serious... can it?

"Yea, I'll take you up on it." I turned and lifted Calvin up from the couch, standing up while he was in my arms. Gemini squealed with aww, Amber laughed and Calvin laid his head on me.

"My hero," he cooed with annoyance, jumping out of my arms. "Gemini next!"

She slowly got up from the couch and shrugged. She put her arms on my shoulders and swung her legs in the air. I caught them easily looking at Amber, but she was staring at Gemini's ass. I put her back down. "Baby?"

Amber got up from the couch. Instead of wrapping her arms around my neck first, she just jumped up and straddled my waist. I caught her ass in my hands with a chuckle. "Did you really want to do the challenge? Or just jump on me?"

She shrugged and hopped down. "Two things can be true. What movie vibe are y'all into tonight? Romance? Comedy? Erotic? Horror?"

Gemini's face changed with erotic. "Not you throwing out porn as a suggestion. I'm cramping, sorry. I don't want to mess up nobody furniture." Amber and I chuckled as Calvin put his head in his hands. "Just saying, it's not because I don't want to."

"Girl," Amber said, trying to slow down her laugh. "You know I have a real good way to help ease those cramps," she said eyeing her.

Gemini smiled and bit her lip, matching her gaze. "I'm listening."

Calvin cheerily reached for the remote on the table. "We can hop into a documentary. I watched a sick one the other day." I gave him a look and moved my eyes back and forth between Amber and Gemini like they didn't make a pass. He took a sip of the margarita Amber made. "Oh this is good! Bae you tried it yet?"

He handed her the glass and she took a sip. "Oh that's nice and cozy. With the sugar on the rim? We see you girl."

Amber sat by Gemini. "I'm glad you liked it. What's your favorite fruit?" she asked her.

"Mangos or strawberries."

Amber went to the kitchen, sliced a couple of Mangos in strips and came back. "I had some in the fridge, you want some?"

"Of course!"

Calvin and I eyed each other. We haven't picked a movie yet, and Amber was already flirting. She sat down and leaned toward Gem, with a slice of mango. "Open up for me."

She licked the side of her lips and opened. Amber placed it just on the tip of her mouth. But instead of taking a bite, Gemini began sucking it, slowly tracing her tongue on the side.

Calvin was staring at her in a daze while I was admiring the burning gaze in Amber's eyes. When Gemini took a bite, Amber ate the rest of it and brushed the side of Gemini's chin with her thumb, painfully slow. "Mmm that was sweet. But I think your lips may be sweeter. Can I kiss you?"

"Yes." Gemini eyed her lips as they both leaned in and kissed. Hearing their lips meet and meet again, watching Amber's face soften. When Gemini lifted her hand to rest it against Amber's neck, it made me exhale deeper. My dick was getting harder by the second, so I turned and began rubbing up and down Calvin's back. He bit his bottom lip, looking back at me.

Gemini pulled back on the kiss. "Mmm. Greg, you never told me Amber would be open to all of us. Did you know Calvin?"

He coughed like he was just pulled out of a trance. "Oh, I mean... kinda."

Gemini nodded looking between Calvin, Amber and me.

"So yall set this up to see if I would be down for a couple swap thing? With Amber and I?"

I pressed my lips together, looking toward Calvin, waiting for him to answer.

"We didn't want to force it between anybody."

She gave Calvin a questioning look. "You know you didn't have to do all of this to get me on board, right? I literally asked you to fuck Greg the first time I met him. Why would you plan this when I'm on my cycle?"

"I wasn't expecting to knock it on early? I thought we had three more days."

The room lightly chuckled. "Mmm. Now I'm horny." Gemini looked at Amber. "Girl, let's plan something. They don't have to be here for us to have fun, but I'm cool with them watching though."

Amber laughed then hugged her, pressing their faces together. "Good," Amber said with the sigh. "Can I kiss you again?"

Gemini laughed and turned her head to her again. This kiss was longer and deeper, Amber straddled Gemini's lap, and I couldn't stop from hitting Calvin on his shoulder in excitement. Amber rolled her hips while Gemini's hands went up and down her back. Calvin just watched them in silence, his eyes focused on Gemini's face, her pleasure, her small moans and whimpers as Amber's hands went up her shirt.

"Damn," Gemini groaned. "Okay hold on a second."

Amber quickly got off her lap, the tense sexual energy in the air split. "I'm sorry."

Gem exhaled loud. "No. You are so good, I'm mad at mother nature right now. Can we smoke? I need to cool off."

I reached under the coffee table and got my rolling tray and sack. "Oh I got that."

Calvin reached in his pocket. "I can get the tray when you're done."

Amber stood up. "Let me go outside and light the fire pit. It's a random warm day, but hell I want to crank it on."

Gemini laughed, standing too. "I'll join you! But, I'm only watching because I don't want to blow nothing up."

Amber roared in laughter. "Yea come on. Just don't be surprised if you look in the window and see Greg and Calvin making out. You know how private they are."

Gem laughed and looked at Calvin. "Mmm hmm they like their privacy, now."

"Okay and?" Calvin questioned with a smile. "I thought this was a safe space."

Gem put her hands up, "You know I'm not trying to get in between nothing. We'll go outside so yall can focus on rolling."

Calvin rolled his eyes as I chuckled, and they walked outside. Gemini is the only person that has watched us together, intimately. Amber has been begging to. It was just different with Gem, everything flowed organically.

Knowing Amber, she was definitely softening Gemini more.

9

AMBER

WE WERE OUTSIDE IN THE BREEZE, GEMINI SITTING IN THE wicker chair, scrolling on her phone, looking sexy as fuck in all black. Her jet black hair was in a fresh twist out that was sitting right under her shoulders. It was easy to light the fire pit, but I wanted to keep the fire between Gemini and I going. I turned on the outdoor speaker, connecting my phone to play *New Feel* by Caterra Joe.

"So," I asked. "You've now kissed a girl, twice. Did you like it?" I grabbed the matchbox, keeping my eyes on her to watch her body language.

She smiled to herself while squeezing her thighs together. "Mmm mm, hell yea. I can't tell you how long I've been wanting to do that. Your lips are so soft. I thought I'd be frozen in place, but I wasn't. This might be TMI, but when you swung your leg and straddled me, my clit started throbbing. That's why I had to stop." She chuckled. "I can't imagine what we could do with me on my... you know."

I struck the match and dropped it into the pit, the fire slowly roared to life. "Oh there is plenty we can do. See with men, that finish one time and that's it. Some keep going, most don't." She rolled her eyes to herself. "But with us, we can go on and on and onnn." I stepped closer to her as she looked up at me.

"On and on?" she questioned.

"Yea, we just keep climaxing until it's over. Sometimes, even hours." Her eyes widened, then softened. "May I sit here?" I said, eying her from her ankles, to her eyes, her lips and back to her expecting eyes.

"Of course." She scooted over. I sat down next to her, our thighs and legs pressed against each other. Then I eased my arm around her shoulder as she leaned against me. "You know, you have a really calming, sexy energy about you."

I laughed to myself. "You do too. I feel like I haven't seen you since your wedding!"

I felt her relax more against me. "Literally. This may be super late, but congrats on your engagement! It was Greg proposing to you before Calvin asked me." She laughed to herself, it was true. "How did he do it?"

I smiled. "He caught me so off guard. We were in Savannah, on a riverboat, I was standing on the railing looking at the water and trees. Then, when I turned around, he was on one knee. I was shocked. We were dating for four years, but still. I was prepared for us to keep living together with no ring anyway. I stood there frozen, he thought I was going to say no. But I started hysterically nodding yes. It was just us, the sound of the water and the big ass ring."

"Can I see it?" she asked.

I stuck out my hand and showed her. I didn't really wear it around the house, but I had it on.

"That's so cute and very you. I love it."

I braced myself for her to ask the usual 5,000 questions. What's the date? Have you sent invitations? Where is it going to be? Do you have a bridal party? But she didn't. We just laid, looking at the fire.

"You're not going to ask me when the wedding is?" I questioned her.

She sat up, meeting my eye. "Do you want me to ask you?"

I blinked, her question caught me off guard. "Um, no I guess not."

Gemini shrugged, "As someone who has planned a wedding, you don't have to do it big with the bells and whistles you know. A wedding is just a big ass party. That's it. The actual ceremony is only like ten minutes, if you rush. You can hire a planner, give a list of what you want, then just show up. The most important thing is you and Greg cause yall are the ones that are tying the knot forever."

Forever.

My heart started to race. Forever? Till death? It's so serious. I can't even imagine what I would do if something happened to him. Then I watched the wheel start turning in her head. Gemini nervously looked away. "Do you feel some type of way because..."

I looked at her with curiosity. "What? What would I feel some type of way about?"

She pressed her lips together. "About me fucking Greg during our threesome?"

I looked at her sideways. "Nah not really. I want to thank you for initiating it, actually."

Her eyes widened. "Huh? Thank me?"

I nodded, "Yea. They wouldn't have opened the door themselves. Greg puts on the tough face, but he's in love with Calvin."

"And Calvin loves Greg back," she finished with an exhale. "I could tell when we were doing it. I literally said, 'yall can kiss if you want.' Then boom, we hit another level. Next thing I know, they were taking turns tearing my shit up."

I clapped and started cheesing. "Yes okay! I'm so jealous. I want to watch them together too."

"I only have that one time. No pictures, no videos, nothing. They'll come around eventually."

Just then, we heard the sliding door open, and they came out laughing.

"It took yall a minute to roll a blunt," Gemini called.

Calvin shrugged. "We got distracted, beautiful. Sorry to make you wait." He bent down and kissed her forehead, then he sat next to Greg on the wicker couch, snuggled next to him. Gemini was still sitting by me. *Maybe this dynamic could work?*

After the smoke break, we finally went back inside. After a vote, everyone decided to watch *Sinners*. Gemini was leaning on my breast while Calvin was rubbing her leg with his head on Gerg's shoulder.

This was peaceful. A great movie, with great people we can trust.

I need to hurry up and pick a date...

10

GREG

WE sat down at our kitchen island with our laptops, opening the bills for next month and reviewing expenses. All bills were able to be paid and then some. The midtown garage needed a new tow truck, more tires, and a few other supplies. Amber had landscaping tools like pavers, gravel and tile on the list for the duplex as well as a legal consultant fee for our lease agreements so they can be reviewed and revised to protect us and what we own. After everything was added, we had enough to take care of what was needed for this month and next. I transferred Amber's "allowance" of 6,000 a month. I didn't want her to work anymore. I hated hearing her complain about the rude guys eyeing her at work, trying to grope her, so she quit.

She spent months applying to jobs. When she was rejected, it would crush her spirit. It would hurt my heart watching her manage the rejection every single day. One day, she had a bad breakdown about wishing to never work again, and I've been wanting to make that wish come true. I gave her ten grand to end her lease and move in with me. I couldn't keep watching her struggle to make ends meet when I genuinely wanted to take care of her and all of her needs. She wouldn't carry my card or ask for money. So she agreed to "earn it" by being a stay at home girlfriend and doing things around the house. Now, she's my fiancée and future wife. I can pay for someone to cook and clean for us, but she says she doesn't need it. Until I see the cleaning crew or chef pull up. I pay them when I see them before she can even sign into the account.

She opened her phone. "You added ten thousand to my personal savings."

"Oh I did?" I faked confusion just to mess with her. "It wasn't a mistake. I want to invest in whatever you want to do. Even if it's leaving me."

She looked shocked. "Leave you? Why would I do that? I love you."

"But not enough to marry me officially."

She huffed. "Okay it's just hard to pick a day, okay! Should it be summer? Fall? Who do we invite and where? We could do a destination wedding or something? Do I even have to wear a white dress? Of course I want to wear white, it's a wedding, but which dress would fit my shape best? A wedding comes with so many questions. Maybe I don't want to be on your schedule."

"I'm thinking about after the wedding, baby. Our family. I want you as my wife. Do you want me to beg? Because I will. Our five-year anniversary is soon, and I want to be yours officially and legally. I'm tired of shacking up witchu."

She rolled her eyes and crossed her arms. "It's not that serious. I'm done talking about it." Then she left the room. I didn't even have time to get down on my knees.

"Be mad, we're still going on our date tonight!" I called as she walked away. I don't care how mad we get, we won't miss our date.

I brushed my beard for the last time in the mirror with Amber posing next to me, obviously posting on her story. I smiled, looking down at her like she was cake fresh out the oven, decadent and soft. After our finance meetings, we always went on a date and switched who planned each one. Sometimes it was a new restaurant or just talking at the park eating wings. Tonight, was my turn to plan. I wanted to give her an excuse to wear the dress I bought her with the slit up her leg. It wasn't too high, but I wanted to rip it off of her.

As we drove over, Johnny Gill was playing on the radio. I lightly poked her arm as she looked at out of the window. "You're not still mad at me are you?"

She shook her head. "No I get it. I didn't realize we were this close to April." She looked at the ring. "I like how we are. I like my girlfriends. You like Calvin and Gemini. Hell, I like them too... I don't want to change. What if I become someone else, and you don't like me anymore?"

I held her hand. "I love you. I want to spend the rest of my life with you. That will never change." I kissed her palm. "Whether if we keep being poly or not. You're my top priority always, my number one."

She smiled and rubbed my hand in hers. "You're my number one too. I couldn't leave you. We have a home together, now more property. I love how we work together, our partnership, relationship. You've always taken care of me and I want to keep taking care of you too. I will be your wife one day. I'll tell you when."

I nodded, keeping my eyes on the road. A part of my heart broke, but I can't rush her. Maybe if I don't bring it up for another five years, she'll decide then.

We went to a late-night event at Georgia Aquarium. There wasn't a big crowd. The lights were dim, so the blues and purples looked like they were dancing on the walls. Amber was in awe. It had been years since we were here, even I forgot how big it was.

We bent the corner, seeing the beautiful colors of the fish

radiating with the light. Amber walked up to the glass wall. I took an off-guard picture of her smiling, her shoulder was lifted to her chin, her fingers down entwined together. I took at least twenty pictures from different angles. I even got in the good squat to cut down the other people in the background. *Yea men can take good pictures.*

I handed her the phone and she wrapped her arm in mine. "Ooo these are cute, now it's your turn."

Fuck, she knows I don't like pictures like that. "Bae you know we don't have to. I saw the sign about the sharks—."

"Gregory, stand up against there. Put your hands in your pockets and keep looking serious with those sexy ass eyes."

I tugged at my beard and looked down to make sure I looked right. I wasn't going to smile, but she made a goofy face and got a small grin. When Amber smiled, it filled her face, showing the mole hidden under her red-painted lips. I kissed the palm of her hand and we continued through the exhibits.

With an alligator swimming above our heads, Amber pulled me to the seat. The area was empty and dark. "Um, I have a question, but don't know if this is the best place to ask."

I squeezed her thigh. "What's up?"

She took a deep breath. "I noticed that we're starting to run low on supplies for your deliveries. Did something happen?"

I rubbed the back of my head, looking away from her. "Well they didn't give me the order. Coraline is working out another deal. If she's not able to, I have someone else I can call."

She nodded. Amber volunteered to pre sack my weed so that it would be easier for me to grab and go or stash in the car. I never asked her to get involved with that "business" but it's not like she didn't know.

After a glass of champagne, watching the sea lions play, and a few more strolls through the exhibits, we were ready to go. Her arm was looped around my shoulder as we walked to the parking garage. She shivered. "Sorry, that wind caught me off guard."

It's February so the temp was still chilly. I quickly took off my peacoat and wrapped it around her shoulders. "Here. You're not about to be cold on my watch."

She looked up at me with a gleam in her eye, then she looked at the ring. "I think I have a date in mind."

————

Amber slammed our front door closed and pushed me against the wall. I love when she's in the mood to take control. I kissed her from her neck, licking the exposed gap between her breasts, down to her stomach. She moaned as my hand came up her thigh, pulling up her dress with me. I was pleased when I met no resistance. "You've been wanting me to eat you up."

"Of course, baby."

I pressed my lips together as I brushed my fingertips up and down her thigh, pushing my bulge against her. "You're lucky I didn't know you had nothing underneath in the car." I moved the open slit of the dress to the side and licked her nipple.

I slowly got on my knees in our entryway. She looked down at me with panting breaths. I lifted her right leg so it was over my shoulder and damn, she tasted amazing. Her sweet lips met mine, expecting me. I started lapping her juices, which made her scratch my waves. I take every one, like a good boy. I slipped my finger inside and her groan bounced off the front door. I could've waited to devour her, but why should I? I wrapped her other leg on my shoulder so her back was on the wall, my hands supporting her ass and waist. My tongue now fucking her clit.

"Fuckkk," she said, pressing her palms into my head. "Babyyy," I twisted my head in the perfect way with my tongue and she splashed my face. Seeing her cream just turned me on more.

"I want more." She whimpered above me.

I guided her down the wall, unbuckling my pants. "I got it for you." I was already stiff, leaking from anticipation. She bent over our entryway table with hooded eyes. I smacked her ass and bent down, holding her open as I licked her pretty clit. "Everything on you is fine baby, fuck." I drew circles with my tip and dove in as she moaned my name.

I need to dig into her shit. I kicked my pants and briefs off, then teased her with my head. She was glistening for me already. I gave her piece by piece, her moans getting lower the deeper I went. I stroked her slow as I held her back down. "You want this, right?"

"Fuck yes, it's yours." I wrapped my arm under her knee so she was hanging in the air as I went faster. The way her ass bounced with my thrust. *Fuck.* It felt so good I kissed her lower back, following my trail of kisses with my thumb. My baby tastes so good.

As my lips met the top of her spine, I reached under and squeezed her nipples. Her breath shuddered under my grasp. I lifted her up, kissing the back of her neck. "I love you so fucking much."

"I love yo-you too, baby." She couldn't focus when I was pounding her back in.

She took a step forward and led me toward the couch under the stairs. She pushed me down, then sat on my lap facing me. I kissed her lipstick-smeared lips. She kissed me back harder, our tongues more than acquainted. She guided me into her and I grunted, lifting my hips forward. Her hands brushed me from my shoulders, down my chest to my belly. She was balanced on her feet, swinging her hips. Feeling her body in the dark was exhilarating. My fiancée. My wife, the future Mrs. Reynolds. I could see her in the wedding dress, her dimples showing as she says I do.

I felt my rise. "I'm gonna c –."

She kissed me, she kissed it out of me as I sprayed her, still rolling on me to catch it all. My shoulders heaved when I finished. After I caught my breath, I got towels for us. We held hands as we walked back into the bedroom. We could leave the mess downstairs for now.

After taking off her makeup, Amber joined me in bed, still naked. Seeing the bathroom light bathe the outline of her thick thighs, I was ready for round two.

She came back into bed with her bonnet on, only. She scooted her ass onto me. I brushed my hand from her knee, up her thighs, past her bellybutton. I loved feeling her body, every mark, every mole.

I rolled on top of her looking down, she opened her legs wider for me and her tight walls greeted me again. Her mouth fell open as she held onto my arms, her nails gently brushing my skin. After a slow kiss, I stroked her faster.

This round was slower, more intense. I could feel the love between dancing in the air. Her beautiful brown eyes never left mine. My lips not leaving her body. We finished at the same time and laid down, tangled in each other.

"I could never feel the way I feel about you with anyone else, Amber. You're the love of my life."

She showed her agreement with a kiss. "I can't wait to show you how much I love you for the rest of our lives."

We went to sleep with my arms wrapped around her, my security blanket.

11

GREG

I PULLED INTO MS. GRANT'S DRIVEWAY. IT'S A RANDOM Thursday morning and she preferred to be discreet. I texted and told her I was outside. I had her order in a backpack since she liked to be set for a while. My supply was getting low, but I could wait a few more days for Coraline to give me an update.

I stood waiting for her to open the door, but it was actually Calvin, who gave me a questioned look.

"Bruh my mom cops from you too? You just get money huh."

I shrugged. "She put in an order, and I delivered it. Did you put in yours?"

His cheeks blushed then he pressed his lips together, opening the door wider. I walked in and saw Gemini scrolling on her phone, probably on *Libby*. Ms. Grant was sitting at the table finishing breakfast. "Gregory honey just sit that on the couch." I did as I was sold and sat it on the couch in the main sitting area.

"How's retirement been treating you?"

She waved me over for a hug and squeezed my shoulders. "It's been good sweetheart. I just might join the Y."

"Well are you going to show up to your 'other' job at the library?" Calvin chimed in. "On top of the car shops."

I crossed my arms and looked at him, he sounded like he missed me. He should know I miss him too. "Yea I was actually headed there after here. Why are you here?" I didn't know where I was headed after this drop off, so Grant Library it was with a fine ass man.

"You don't get to ask me why I'm at my mama's house."

Gemini yelled, eyes still on her phone. "We stayed the night, our townhouse lost heat."

Calvin made a face at me that made me laugh. He's just so damn nerdy, fine and annoying. "I bet I'll beat you there."

"I'm walking to my car now." I walked back through the living room, "Bye Ms. Grant, see yall later alright?"

"Bye sweetheart, tell Amber I said hello and I'm still expecting a wedding invitation."

"Yes ma'am." I waved to Gemini and she nodded back. When I turned around, Calvin was headed to his room to probably get dressed. He didn't want to race and knew I would beat him.

"WELL YOU'RE NOT ON TIME, BOSS MAN," I YELLED ACROSS THE parking lot.

Calvin scoffed. "We have multiple copies of keys, you don't have to wait for me." We chuckled, shoving each other as we passed the front doors. I greeted everyone as I took a seat behind the counter. This was really why I liked coming here. It didn't feel like anywhere else.

Growing up, I went to the library to get away from everything. On the off chance Bull wasn't looking for me to work, I was at the library. Finding albums, reading books I never even thought of. That's why I require book reports along with the scholarship application, and I screen them for AI usage. The generations after me need to be able to have a choice on the life they want, but reading is a requirement and necessity.

I noticed new blue couches in the sitting area by the window. We texted the other week and he said they received a big donation from an anonymous donor, he was able to get a new couch for upstairs and downstairs and he saved the rest. I was proud of him.

He sat down next to me, signing into the computer. "So," I started. "I notice the new couches."

"Yea I told you about that. The blue looks good next to the carpet. Right?"

"It looks nice." I took my voice down a few notches and leaned close to his ear. "You and wifey broke them in yet? I know y'all are tired of the desks."

His face scrunched tight as he slapped my arm. "You looked at the cameras again didn't you."

Now my eyes were wide. "I was just joking, y'all are nasty as fuck. I learned my lesson on seeing why the doors were opened late at night."

A group of elderly women walked in, we waved hello and smiled as they walked past. He chuckled as we nudged each other.

After registering two library cards and showing three people how to use the printer, I checked my watch and it was now noon. I wanted lunch, but something told me to wait. Then I saw a familiar face walk in through the door.

Is that Demetrius?

He had the same walk he had in middle school, but his face aged and he had a tear tattoo under his right eye. His neck covered in ink.

"Yo its D. I haven't seen you in a minute."

"Yea, yea I've been low-key. I stopped by the car shop and you weren't there so I figured you were here, Greg. I hope the fams been good." He rocked side to side, holding his hands.

That was not a good sign. He was really looking for me. "Yea, yea we've been straight. Yours? Your baby mama glad you back?"

He sucked his teeth. "She aight. I gotta move out of that spot soon. Y'all hiring here?"

I sized him up, still trying to be friendly. "Nah, we're fully staffed, but we'll take your resume."

He made a show of checking his pockets. "I don't even have one on me." He tapped the counter. "I'll be sure to come back." He dapped me up and walked out looking around.

Calvin walked up, notebook in hand. "Was that D? In Cobb? I didn't know he was out."

"Yea, asked for a job." I spun in the chair to face him. "You know that's not a good sign."

He nodded. "Yea I know."

I blew raspberries walking back to Calvin's office as he followed and closed the door. "It might not be that serious. He could've just pulled over."

"He went by the shop. He wanted to make sure I knew he was there. Then asked about my fam. This is not good and he shouldn't be on this side anyway."

"Well don't make it worse. Take the resume, even if it calms down the front. He may never come back."

I rubbed my temples. "Shit." He walked over, and sat in the chair next to me. He placed his hand on my knee. I placed my hand on top of his and took a deep breath, trying to hide the anger rising in my chest. This was a safe space, so how did he know about it just after being released? Someone sent him here, *probably Marcus still mad we didn't take his deal.*

"Hey, look at me," Calvin said. "Everything will be okay. We've got cameras, nobody has done anything here before. Did something bad happen?"

We locked eyes. "Yea."

He sighed. "Still, the Grant name is on the building. I may not know much. But I know people don't fuck with us much."

"But I'm not a 'Grant.' I'm Greg *Reynolds*." I wiped my hand down my face. "I'm gonna head out and sit in the parking lot for a minute to clear my head."

"You mean roll a blunt," he said teasingly.

I made a face and tapped the counter. "I'll hit you up later." We fist bumped and I walked out the door. I just needed a minute to clear my head. Seeing Demetrius was like watching your tombstone get built. And he was looking for me.

I moved my car from the entrance and backed into a spot in the cut under some trees. It was cold not being in the sun, but I was straight. I rolled the blunt, scanning the lot.

D was gone.

I was halfway through the blunt, staring at the duplex cameras to spot any familiar cars when "Future Wifey" pops up as a FaceTime. I answered trying to not look pissed and uneasy.

"Hey baby! I'm at the nail salon." She did a scan of the place behind her.

"You need some bread?" I asked.

"Nah I'm good. But I need help picking a color." She flipped the screen to show two pink nail polishes in her hand. "I can't decide between Passion Pink and Girls Wanna Have Fuchsia. Which one?"

I was genuinely confused, they looked like the same color. This is the indecisive Libra shit I've been talking about.

"Don't say, 'they look the same' because they don't. One has a richer, darker tone."

I shook my head and pulled from the blunt. "The one on the right, it looks brighter?"

She squealed. "Yay! I was hoping you would pick that one. I secretly wanted it."

I blew out the smoke nodding, looking out the window.

"You okay? You seem distracted. Where you at?"

"I was just choppin' it up with Calvin, about to do some orders then go home."

"Okay baby, see you at home."

"I love you. I need you to know that I want to spend the rest of my life with you. I'll love you forever. You hear me?"

Her eyebrow twisted. "Yes, I hear you babe... I love you too. Is something wrong? What happened?"

I closed my eyes and took a deep breath. Amber knew Demetrius, he was a regular at Green Envy Gentleman's Club when she was a bottle girl. He was never friendly and was known for catching bodies like a Venus fly trap gets flies. "Nothing. Enjoy your nail appointment. I'll see you at home." Hopefully.

"Okay," she looked at me like she knew something was wrong. "I'm headed home after my appointment and I'm expecting to see you there."

"I'll be there baby, love you."

She said it back and ended the call. I breathed knowing that she was okay and wasn't at the duplex. What if someone was watching her? Tailing us?

Fuck the orders, I don't feel like serving shit right now. I quickly sped out of the parking lot and made my way home, the long way.

The first thing I did was check our safes for the weapons. There was one in every room of the house that would only open to Amber's or my fingerprint. Everything was accounted for. I'd hate for shit to pop off in my house, but you never knew with Deadly Demetrius.

Amber came through the front door with Gucci shades, sapphire blue, waist-high leggings and a jacket. "I thought I heard you come in ahead of me. You just got here?" She asked, putting down her keys.

I opened my arms. "Yea I took the long way." She lifted her head and kissed me, giving me a kiss that eased and lowered my shoulders from the tension I've been holding all day. I kissed her back deeper, squeezing and lifting her ass. "Mmm, you can't be kissing me like that."

She playfully swatted my shoulder. "I can kiss you however I want, I missed you." She eyed me up and down with a smize. "Are you going to tell me why you've been acting weird?"

"I have something to tell you," I said.

Her face fell.

"Nothing bad, I promise."

Her face was more confused. "People usually say that before saying something bad. Spit it out."

I rubbed my beard, looking away from her, "The drop off and pick up from a while ago didn't go as planned. I thought it would be good but... it's not. Demetrius came by the library looking for me. I'm pretty sure Marcus sent him."

Her entire face moved as she took a step back. "Demetrius, as in Dead if you see me D? Fuck that."

She moved from my arms and ran upstairs. By the time I caught up to her, she was pulling cash out of the safe in our closet. "Nope, hell nah. We need to get out of here. Now."

"Baby I can't quit yet. And even if I do, I'd need to open another shop and that takes bread. We don't even have tenants in the duplex yet. Who would run it if we left? We'd look crazy to sell it and it'd be for cheap since we're in the middle of renovations. I want a legacy in this city. Whether it's the school kids, creating jobs or affordable housing. We can have it."

"What about me, huh?" She looked at me with pain in her eyes. "What about me?"

I swallowed. "You know how to get to my life insurance. I don't think he even wants to hurt you."

She waved her arms in the air. "Here you go again with that. I can't live without you Gregory! They can kill me too! I don't have shit. Not a business, not your last name. Nothing! I would leave this Earth with nothing. If D is involved, then we're already fucked. You know that. Why did Bull have to get those kids shot, all because Casey was in the wrong room at the wrong time? It was so random. You know one of them was a sophomore at Morehouse?" She threw her clothes in a different gym bag. "He played basketball, trying to do some gang shit he knew nothing about. And now look."

She paused, holding her leggings with shaky hands. "You don't understand how worried–" She gasped. "How worried I get when you leave. You're my safety, you're my security. So let's go while we have the chance."

She was running around the room a mile a minute. Throwing both of our clothes in suitcases, getting the guns packed in a travel safe and briefcase. As she was starting to pack her pants, my voice barely came through.

"I can't leave. What about the library? And Cal..."

She blew air out of her mouth. "You know this is part of the life. He may need to lay low too."

"What about our house? Our home? That loan is in our name. We have a mortgage."

She dug in the closet and picked through the money bag then threw it at me. I caught it in my arms. "Here. Pay the house off and keep it. But I won't be in it."

I dropped it and grabbed her hand. "The feds would be onto us faster than white on rice. We need just a little more time." She shoved me away and went into the closet safe again, taking out our documents. She opened both of our passports and nodded.

"What are you doing?" I asked.

"Making sure our passports haven't expired yet."

Now I was pacing the room, *shit*. I know the order didn't go as planned. It could've just been to scare me. People know Calvin has owned that library for years now. He was in the newspapers when it was saved. He was never a part of the drug life. I loved him, but I love Amber more. She's my future wife. I'm not going anywhere until she has my last name. "Pick a date and marry me, Amber."

She looked at me then took out her phone, opening her calendar. "Next Friday the 20th of February."

That was ten days away. We had ten days to plan our wedding.

"Can we even get a license that fast?"

"I'll look and see." She quickly pulled her laptop from the nightstand and opened it. After clicking for a few minutes, she said, "Our license appointment is Monday. So we'll technically be married in less than a week."

I stood still in shock. I realized I hadn't taken a step since we started the conversation in the bedroom. I slowly walked over to her and lifted her chin. What I've been waiting on, she's finally decided. She chose me. "You're going to be my wife."

"And your annoying ass is going to be my husband. You really said you didn't want to leave Calvin. I caught that. You really like that nigga. Like, you're really in love. I'm a little jealous because of the history you two have. I know it's different but still. But, I get it. You realize that if we don't leave the country, we could be dead in a week. Fucking hell."

I wrapped her in my arms and kissed her cheek. "You know, you're sexy when you're mad and mean."

She lightly shoved me. "Oh I can be a lot of things when I'm mad."

Amber smiled but got serious again. She stopped packing but I could see her mind spinning. I didn't need her to worry about a plan, I had us. "Now I get to go tux hunting."

She groaned loud. "FUCK I need a dress." She pulled a wad of cash out of the bag. "This is for the dress and pain and suffering."

"What's mine is yours."

She walked away annoyed, but I was suddenly excited. Could our lives be ending?

Maybe.

Will I see Amber walk down the aisle in a white dress with white roses at our feet?

I hope so.

12

AMBER

Since Greg and I have now set a date for our wedding, I guess I need a dress and all the things that come with that. I don't even know who to call for fashion advice. I don't have real friends here. Bitches I can call when I want to get drunk? Yes because they would beat me there to get in free. Girlfriends to lay in bed and cuddle with? Duh. I have my roster.

But no one for wedding dress fittings, and planning a wedding for next Friday. We have eight days. Greg works too many places to plan it, so here I go. I texted the only other married woman I know.

Me: Guess who's going wedding dress shopping tomorrow?

Gemini: Ooo who?

Me:

Gemini: Ahhh! I can't wait. Congrats! I've been dying to go to a wedding I didn't plan 🥹😍

Me: Well you might be helping do it again

Gemini: Count me in!

THAT SATURDAY WE ONLY WENT TO TWO STORES BECAUSE I WAS scared I'd change my mind too many times. Gemini and I looked through multiple racks. "Who came with you to your dress fitting?" I asked her.

"Aunt Lorraine. I wanted Casey there, but she was out of town. But that was it." She shrugged and kept looking.

I paused and looked at her. "I thought your mom lived here?"

She shook her head. "The closest thing I have to a 'real' mom is Lorraine. To be real."

I nodded. "My parents abandoned me when I was a baby. If my neighbor didn't call for a welfare check... I would've died. She chose to adopt me after that."

She wrapped me in a hug and squeezed. "Chosen family, right?"

"Right," I agreed. Emotion was rising in my throat, but I pretended something was in my eye. After trying on five dresses, I found the one that made my titties look perfect while showing off the rose tattoo that crept up my rib.

I stepped out onto the platform and turned to Gemini and the staff. "Yo, this is real... I'm actually marrying Gregory."

"Yes, yes you are. Do you want to? Because if you don't or you change your mind you can tap me at any point and we can run. I will have the Uber outside ready for us."

I busted out laughing. "I picked the date and basically the

reason why we're doing it at the last minute. This is the dress, I feel it."

Gemini looked at me like she was about to cry. "Oh, Greg will be crying at the altar when he sees you in this. Turn around, it snatched your waist right up, girl."

I moved the train and admired myself in the mirror again. "You think so?"

Gemini stood up and placed her hands on my shoulder. "I know so... now ring that bell!"

I rang the bell in my hand and jumped up and down as everyone cheered, "you said yes to the dress." It was happening. I was alive another day so D hadn't found us again. I should've married Greg six months ago, but here we are. I want to be his wife. Demetris just lit a fire under my ass threatening to kill him.

I FOUND A MICRO WEDDING PLANNER THAT AGREED TO MEET WITH us virtually. The appointment was at 8:00 a.m. Sunday morning. Greg was up before me, getting dressed so we could make a good impression. When we turned on the camera, she had an old school crimp hair style, she looked organized. She had a venue she owned that overlooked I-85 and a green space if we wanted to be on a lawn. She was within our quick turnaround budget and could get started immediately since the big day was now five days away. She emailed us the pictures. I asked if we could confirm with her tomorrow and she agreed to twenty-four hours.

She ended the call as we continued to look through the twenty picture slide show of the room and balcony that was empty then for seating with 30 and 10 people. "Do you think we could get away with having ten people there? We aren't broke," I said with a nudge.

"I thought you were tired of waiting, Mr. Gimmie a date."

Greg laughed. "If you want 'leave the country money' then the least amount of people there, the better. You can legally have my last name tomorrow, so I'm just focused on that. Right after the ceremony, I'll help you change your name on everything... as long as you want to."

I leaned up on my toes and kissed him, running my fingers through his bearded chin. "Of course I want the new name immediately, baby. I've been ready a long time too. That's why I sign my little notes with Mrs. Reynolds so I can practice."

Once again, Gregory cleared his schedule so we could go to the courthouse for our marriage license. After confirming we have no living spouse and signing a couple of documents. We had the license.

Then we found out we weren't officially married until we had some sort of ceremony that was officiated and signed. He was upset but I tried to make him smile with the fact that we were four days away from our big day. I emailed the wedding planner a secret picture of my dress, and emphasized again that white roses were mandatory. She said she could make it all happen since we paid the full amount early, including a two-tiered vanilla cake.

We got back in my car. Greg got behind the wheel because, where else? He looked at the lights near the gas level. "When was the last time you took your car by the shop?"

I shrugged. "I don't know. I've been busy."

Gregory sighed loud. "Let's get your car back to the crib so I can look at it."

At the house, my car was in the garage with the hood up. He was checking every nook, corner, pipe, and level. "Alright, your oil needs to be changed so imma do that. Your coolant is good. I'll rotate your tires too because you need it and because I like you, I'll even clean and switch out your cabin air filter."

I shivered my shoulders. "Couldn't Take 5 do the same thing?"

He turned around so fast I thought his neck broke. I just like to piss him off. "Take 5? Not even to the repair shop? Damn did we do something? So you want to pay an extra $250. You know you're good with me. Quit playing. No other man is touching your car but me."

As he mumbled to himself, I rubbed his back. "Want some water or a smoothie? Since my man is working hard out here."

"I'll just have a water. It's a little cold for a smoothie." I shrugged and made both. I sat in the garage and watched him work. There was nothing sexier than seeing a man bent over putting air in your tires, drenched in sweat, blasting hype ass music.

He takes such good care of me.

After he finished and took a shower, we sat on the bed and watched music videos. When I lay my head on him, my brain goes quiet. I don't have to think or worry because I know he got it.

He got me. Even if it felt like death was right around the corner, watching us.

13

___

CALVIN

I was on the second floor of the library with Indys Blu playing in one ear, and recommending *Finding Me* by Viola Davis when I heard pages flapping downstairs. I ignored it at first, but kept hearing it. *What is going on?*

"Aye bitch, I already asked you if Greg was here."

"I don't know!"

The fuck?

I excused myself, pulled out my headphone and quickly got to the ledge, looking over the railing. Demetrius and two other guys were yanking books off the shelves downstairs and throwing them on the ground. I was not about to wait on the elevator. I threw open the door and sped down the stairs. My knees and feet moving faster than my mind.

When I made it to the first floor, I put on a fake smile. "Demetrius! You came back with friends. Is there a book I can help you find?"

He walked up to me with a fake smile, his neck tattoos flexing. "Greg here fam?"

"Nah he's not. So I am going to ask you to leave. We've got kids here man. I don't want any trouble." I started walking toward the door, hoping he'd follow. When I glanced behind me, he and his crew weren't far.

When we were in the lobby, it was empty but it had an echo. "Ion wanna come back here no more Calvin. I fuck with you, but don't fuck with that fat nigga. He owes my partner money. That's the only reason I'm leaving, aight?"

"Alright."

He shoved his shoulder past mine, walking by. "Here's a message." Then he kicked the glass next to the door handle, causing it to shatter on the floor. The hole was big and everyone else was looking concerned and confused. As they quickly made their exit.

"Everything is okay. I'm calling a glass repairman." I hope his quote isn't more than $500 or it won't be good the next few months. I told my team to walk around and check on everyone to make sure they're okay and reassure that everything was fine and safe.

———

WHEN I MADE IT HOME TO THE TOWNHOUSE, GEMINI WAS ON HER laptop at the kitchen island. I already told her about what happened and to keep it a secret. She thought I should give Greg the heads-up. But I don't want him thinking about this before his wedding. I'll tell him after and it'll be cool.

Reeooow.

"Hey Constance." Our black cat brushed her head against my legs and walked in circles meowing louder. "Hey Gem!"

She was so zoned in on her laptop that she didn't even look at me. I walked over and put my arm around her back and she jumped. "Damnit fuck," she yelped then came closer. "Sorry didn't realize it was you. Do you know the charges this man was released for? It was two charges of voluntary manslaughter and larceny. Like excuse me? At that age? If I were Greg, I wouldn't go back there at all. Demetrius, D, whoever doesn't seem like a 'let's sit down and talk about it' kind of guy. He's who you call when you want somebody dead."

I hugged her tight. "We don't need to go there right now. I can't think about it."

Her face softened as her eyes shined with understanding. "Do you want to hear how horrible my day was?"

I leaned against the island, admiring her. "Of course, lay it on me."

She took a deep breath. "Would you believe the name they picked for this fucking AI that's supposed to do all these great things, but it just keeps freezing. The name is Helpi. What kind of name is that? HELPI! The company is already called Helping Human Helpers, so now Helpi is helping humans help each other *through* artificial intelligence. Whatever, stupid ass AI, fuck. I don't even care anymore, but if I have to look at this useless ass question mark wearing a hard hat dance one more time at the bottom of the screen, rather than give the answer I told it to give, I'm going to curse out every single software developer and person on my team. They should give me a fucking raise for everything that I've been doing on this project for the last few months. It's like I came back from being off on our honeymoon and they just threw me in head first, like man could I at least get a pat on the back or something? Instead of denying ALL of my time off requests?"

I nodded, they were putting additional pressure on her. "I'm sorry baby. When will the project be over?"

She sighed louder and closed the laptop. "I don't know. They keep pushing the go live date. It's changed four times already."

I opened my arms and she dropped her head on my chest as I rubbed her back in a tight hug. "It's okay."

"The team in California doesn't take me serious at all. That's what pisses me off most."

I looked at her and kissed her cheek. "Fuck them."

She nodded, lifting her head up. "Yea... yea! Fuck them. I'm not letting them have any more of my time tonight. People will still call HR and ask us how it works." She took another deep breath. "I hate that Greg has hot shit following him. I hope him and Amber stay safe. The wedding is so close and we already got her dress. I'm nervous as fuck now. What would Amber do if she lost him? What would that do to you?"

I looked her in the eye and brushed my thumb across her cheek. "I don't know. If I lost you Gem, I'd be a shell. I hope they stay safe too. Let's keep our phones close and on just in case."

She agreed and we sat on the couch, watching a show where the homeowner definitely picked an ugly color for the walls. Trying to take our mind off the real world. I can't imagine a world without my best friend, my partner.

A man I've loved for years.

14

GREG

As soon as I walked in, the other librarians were giving me a weird look, like they were scared. Did something happen when I wasn't here? I approached Calvin in his office. Everyone was usually cool with me and spoke, but they avoided my glance as I walked to the back.

"Has Demetrius been back here?"

Calvin sighed. "Yea. But it was three of them. I didn't recognize who he was with. They broke the door, but it's fixed now."

What the fuck! He fucked up the door that bad! What if it was worse? "Damn why didn't you tell me?"

"Your wedding is days away. The day you've been waiting almost five years for. I know wedding planning isn't easy, especially this cut for time. I wasn't going to worry you about this."

I sighed. I didn't have cold feet, I just had a bad feeling. Something was lingering that I couldn't place my fingers on. For safety, we agreed to invite ten people. Not enough people? Fuck. I barely got my tux fit in time. I was not going to look crazy on the best day of my life. We didn't need 300 people with chocolate fountains and doves released through the sky.

Calvin stood up and braced his hands on my shoulders.

"Man, you got this. You've been obsessed with Amber since forever. You know she's the one for you. It's all this other shit going on."

I nodded. "You're right. D coming by really shook me up. I never wanted to cause anyone trouble. This fucking hot shit keeps following me and I don't want my loved one getting hurt." Then my phone rang, it was bae. I sighed to myself and answered. Before I could respond she screamed in my ear.

"I got my dress! I'm so excited I can't believe the big day is tomorrow. They did a rush on the alterations so it could get done on time. Offering the $300 tip helped too, but still."

I smiled at her excitement. I didn't know if she would have time to get a real dress, but I'm glad she did. My stomach started to tighten from the mix of anxiety and anger boiling together. "Can I call you back?"

"Yea of course! Is everything okay?"

I'm not telling her D came back or she'd want to fly out tonight. Even though we probably should. "Yea I just stubbed my toe on a bookshelf. That shit hurt."

"Aww, I'm sorry. We'll look at it when you get home. Will you be gone long? I know the big day is tomorrow, but I want to spend the night with you."

Calvin glanced at me, then looked back down trying to hide his own worry.

"I'm headed back to the house now. The library is doing good."

Everything was not good.

I hugged Calvin then quickly left with my head down and on a swivel.

While I was driving, Coraline called and I answered quickly.

"I hope you have some good news," I said hopefully.

"I don't. Everything is hot right now. We both need to lay

low. My family should be okay, your family is the one I'm worried about."

I heard keyboard clacks behind me. "D came by the library again looking for me. Your brother didn't tell me until today."

"I know. He knows damn well to stay out of Cobb county. I tried to connect with four people with no luck. If I smell fish or a rat, I don't go. I'm sorry, but when you're out, you're out. You'll have to use another connect."

I squeezed the wheel. I'm down to a zip, then I'm out. No more orders, no more second income. "We'll be good. Don't worry about us Coraline."

Then an eerie silence came on her line.

"Coraline? Are you good?"

She sighed. "Yea I'm just trying to put a plan together. You just lay low. I'll see you at the wedding."

"See you then."

Then she ended the call. When Coraline was nervous, that's when I was on extra alert. She's always been three steps ahead. She's been worried about her family most of her life, she doesn't need to add me to that. I've got my own family to protect.

I kept checking my rearview as I drove. My house was the safest place I had, that location can't be given to anyone I don't personally trust.

WHEN I MADE IT HOME, AMBER HOPPED IN THE CAR NOT EVEN asking where we're going. So I just drove. I drove to clear my head because I can't tell her how bad everything actually was days before our wedding. I was starving and pulled into the McDonald's on MLK Drive.

"You don't need to eat this the night before our wedding. Your skin looks great and I don't want you to ruin it."

I playfully rolled my eyes. "Just something real quick to

hold me before I start cooking dinner. I meant to grab lunch after leaving the midtown location and forgot."

"See this is why I make your lunch, because you go around to everyone else, driving all around the city without something on your stomach, then wonder why you're starving with a headache at five o'clock."

I pulled up to the window, scanning the menu. The car in front of me slammed on their breaks. I thought they were just grabbing their food.

As I turned to speak in the speaker, reverse lights hit my peripheral, Amber was on her phone looking down.

I laid my hand on the horn as she gasped, looking up. The car was headed right for us with rearview lights on bright.

HHHOOONNNNKKKK!

They weren't going to stop.

As I was stretching my arm across Amber -

"GREGORY!" *BAM!*

They hit my car so hard I heard the bumper crumble and some glass break. The car shook on impact.

Amber jerked back, holding her forehead. My arm bounced off her chest. I heard her head hit the seat, so she may have gotten whiplash. I was able to brace for it, but nothing hurt right now. My chest was getting hot from the rising anger.

They fucked up fucking with me.

I reached under my seat, feeling for my gun. "No matter what stay in the car, okay?"

She groaned, holding the front of her head.

I checked to make sure it was loaded. "Baby you heard me?"

"Huh?" She groaned again, leaning her head against the window. She looked bad. I needed to get her to the hospital.

"Amber, Amber baby stay awake, please." I put the gun back under the seat. The car was already gone, but I remembered the county and license plate.

UJE4Y Decatur

They were gonna pay.

I revved my engine to make sure the car would work. Then drove out of the line headed to Grady, trying to get my baby to stay awake. I called Calvin as I was driving to meet us there. He said he'd beat me and wait in the lobby.

They brought out a wheelchair for her as they helped her onto it. One of the nurses yelled that she was in critical condition and rushed Amber to the back past the reception desk, my hands were folded behind my head, following the EMS and stretcher. Right before I passed the threshold of doors, a hand touched my shoulder. "Excuse me sir, are you a family member?"

I sneered, he looked young in the face, probably a college kid or young nurse wanna be. "She's my fiancé, so yes."

The jit in green scrubs face twisted. "She's being assessed by the doctor now. We can't let anyone be present for that in case she will need to be rushed to surgery or need further examination. Since we don't have an empty room right now for you to wait in. We'll take care of her, but you'll have to wait in the waiting room until the doctor gets you."

My fear is coming true.

"Are you fucking serious?"

"Yes sir." He gave me the look I was used to, the "I'll call security if you don't turn around" face.

I turned on my heel and headed for the glass exit doors. *Fuck.* FUCK! I should've punched the fucker.

Calvin was jogging behind me to catch up. "Wait!"

I walked outside. I didn't know if I wanted to punch a wall or kick rocks on the ground. How could I have let this happen? What could I have done so that my baby girl wouldn't be on a stretcher right now?

Calvin came up behind me and put his hand on my back. "What did they say? I know this is rough..."

I could barely hear him as my ears were ringing, what if she didn't walk out of the room? What if I waited too long for her to set a date? If we were married last week or months ago, I would be in the room with her, but our date is tomorrow and one day made a difference. She could be paralyzed. *This is all my fault.*

Calvin rubbed circles on my back. I tried to slow down my breathing, but I can't imagine a life without her. Without my wife. I covered my face with my hands and cried. It wasn't a slow cry. It was a bitter cry. A wail grew in my throat that I couldn't swallow.

He wrapped his arms around me and gave me a hug as I hugged him back, my head bent down and nestled in his shoulder. I felt so weak that I could drop to my knees. I deserved to be on the stretcher, not her. I was trying to protect her. It felt good to release what I was holding. My chest was already starting to feel looser. I was still scared, but at least Calvin was here with me. The tears started to slow, and my breath was coming back to me.

"How could I have let this happen? How could I have let this happen?" I kept whimpering.

"It's not your fault. I'm sure they have cameras in the drive-thru. Let the cops handle that, not you. You are not Bull. Amber needs you, bruh. I need you. We got you."

He started rocking side to side as I rocked with him.

After a long moment, I pulled back and used my fist to wipe my face. "I'm a fucking punk to be crying in public."

Calvin pushed my chest. "No you're not. This is a hospital, they're used to niggas crying. I'll get you some tissues."

When he went inside, I took three shaky deep breaths. I needed to get myself together. Atlanta is too small, can't get word going around about me and Calvin. I'm not ready for that yet.

"Here you go." He handed me the tissue, and I wiped my face again and blew my nose.

"I'm good now. Let's get back to the waiting area."

He rubbed my arm. Gemini saved seats in the corner by the chargers. When we got closer, she looked up and stood and hugged me tight. "It'll be okay. Do you need to be checked out? You were in the car too."

"Nah I'm good, my back is just a little sore."

She frowned. "They could give you something for the pain, Greg."

I shook my head and sat down. She squeezed my shoulder and sat back down too.

Now we wait.

15

GREG

After three hours, I was getting nauseous. *What is taking them so fucking long?* I stood up, headed to registration again for an update, *again*.

"Is anyone here with Amber Cress?"

I turned my head so fast I felt a twinge. A man in white coat said scanning the waiting room.

"Yes, we are," I said as Calvin and Gemini stood up next to me.

The doctor came back toward us, then offered a sitting room with a table and a few chairs. Calvin and Gemini sat back down. I nodded to them not to leave yet. I was nervous he was going to tell me she was dead, so I wouldn't let my mind go there. *Listen, just listen to what he says.*

"Are you Gregory?" he asked.

"I am. She's my fiancée."

He nodded. "She's been asking for you. Her tests came back clear, but she does have significant head and back trauma. She was in pain from the whiplash but she's better now since we gave her something to help. She may seem frazzled for the next couple of days. I understand you all are getting married tomorrow?"

"Yes sir. She finally agreed on the date."

The doctor's lips moved. "I would highly recommend against it. She should be resting. There are no bruises, but weddings tend to bring a lot of stress that could worsen her symptoms. I'm prescribing her ibuprofen to help with the pain at home, it may increase over the next few days as the adrenaline wears off. She might even be loopy or lose some memory from the accident. Just think about how she would look in the photos, you know? Besides the pain, she'll not be herself for a few days, so just be mindful of that."

I nodded, but the date has been set. I've waited years for tomorrow and won't wait longer. What if something worse happens from today until tomorrow? Either D or Marcus, from the deal that didn't happen, had something to do with it. They could be working together. Nobody knows the address of my house, and I wasn't taking any chances.

"Were you in the car too? Are you in any pain?"

I shook my head. My neck ached, but I can stretch it out. "Nah I'm good. I can take care of myself. Can I take her home now?"

The doctor stood up, so did I. "Yes as soon as we finish her discharge paperwork. We sent her prescription to our pharmacist, so it should be ready in ten minutes or less. Any other questions?"

We walked out of the room. "No that was it. Thank you, doctor," I said with an extended hand.

He shook my hand. "You're welcome. You can come back and see her now."

I glanced at Calvin and Gemini, reading in the break area. "Please."

I've never seen Amber in a hospital. I thought the first time I would it would be for pregnancy appointments, not because a bitch ass nigga recognized my car in a drive-thru. I smiled seeing her sitting up, squinting at her phone. *In sickness and in health, for better or worse.*

"Gregory." She opened her arms and I ran into them. I hated seeing her with the wires and tubes around her. I nuzzled my nose against her neck, trying to swallow my tears. I kept holding her, not squeezing too tight. "Stop worrying, I'm fine. They said I can leave soon. We're just waiting on my prescription and the paperwork."

I pulled back, feeling somber. "Maybe I would've been back here sooner if we were married."

She rolled her eyes. "Yes the same argument we've been having, I know, I know. But I'm okay. I'll get to go home, we can get married tomorrow and everything. My face isn't swollen or anything. At least glass didn't break."

I sighed. Seeing her in the hospital bed made me change my mind. Maybe we should push the date. I don't want her drugged up or even forgetting the wedding because of the accident. "Maybe we should push the date a few weeks. The doctor said you'd be in pain and -."

"Don't do that! I want to get married tomorrow, no matter what. We don't have to go on a honeymoon or anything, but I can walk, so I'm standing at somebody's altar to marry you tomorrow. I don't fucking care."

I brushed my hand against her face. "Okay, baby. Whatever you want."

The nurse came in with the discharge instructions, Amber's prescription and a wheelchair.

"I'm not getting in that." Amber said matter a fact. "I can walk. I'm fine."

The nurse sighed to herself but smiled. "Miss you came in critical condition. You can practice walking at home. According to our policy, you have to be wheeled out, due to the state you came in so we can safely get you to your vehicle."

Amber crossed her arms and swung her legs back on the bed. "I'll tell the doctor I won't leave then. I want to walk."

The nurse put her hand on her hip. "I'll get you the waiver so you can walk back to the parking garage."

I gently touched Amber's hand. "You know you don't have to be prideful right? We can practice at home. But if you fall again, then you would definitely be here another day." I gave her a meaningful look in her eye. "I don't want anything to happen."

She sighed as she got up from the bed and into the chair. "I'm so embarrassed."

"You don't need to be," I encouraged. "We were hit head-on and it's a policy." I gathered her bag from the chair in the corner. The nurse put the breaks on the chair as Amber slowly lowered herself down.

"Ready?" the nurse asked.

I nodded. She released the break and backed out of the room with me behind them. Amber's chin rested in her palm as we weaved through the halls.

When we walked past the lobby, Amber saw Calvin and Gemini. She looked surprised to see them as she smiled to herself. Then did a small shy wave. The nurse wheeled her over to them.

"Wow you guys came? It was only a small accident."

Gemini stood up and stretched. "Girl that was not small. You didn't see how they rushed you back there. We wanted to make sure you were okay." Then she bent down and hugged Amber.

"I can take her the rest of the way, thank you," I told the nurse.

"You're welcome!" she said, putting on the breaks, then handing me the paperwork and prescription. "Get home safe!" she called, and I wished her the same.

"We can follow you home too," Calvin added. "We're not taking no for an answer."

I nodded, not putting up a fight. It was at least two in the morning, and they were willing to still follow us home to make sure we were both okay. Safe.

This is our family.

AFTER AMBER WAS IN BED, I TEXTED THE WEDDING PLANNER TO ask if our home could be the new wedding venue. Only Calvin, Gemini, Coraline, Casey, Denver, Ms. Grant, Amber's girlfriends, and Monte were coming anyway. Everyone coming was a part of our circle that meant more to us than life. We need to be safe to not only protect us, but everyone we love and care for. I can't have any funny shit.

The wedding planner said she could move everything to our home and set it up in the backyard and living room for an extra fee. I sent her the money immediately, and she thanked me. Gemini yawned when I came back into the kitchen. "Y'all go home, man and get some rest."

Calvin put his hand on my arm. "What about tomorrow? Well I guess tonight."

"Plan to come here, same time but different place. We need to lock down. I need a security detail too." I wiped my face. "Today has been long. I can't even think anymore."

Gemini stood on my other side and put her hand on my shoulder. "Take a shower, try to stretch and relax, then lay in bed with Amber. Let us do whatever we can tomorrow to help. We'll handle security, where everything is going and all that. Amber is your priority. Okay?"

"Yea man," Calvin added. "The day you've been waiting for is officially here. Try to enjoy it and we'll do everything we can.

"Aight, thank yall."

"Of course, you're important to us too, you know." She smiled and hugged me. "We'll see you later."

Gemini started walking toward the car and Calvin stayed back. He gave me the look in his eye where he didn't have to say more. I wrapped him in a tight hug and he squeezed back.

"Take a deep breath."

I inhaled through my nose and blew it out.

"Good. We'll be back soon." As Calvin pulled away, I squeezed his ass as he laughed.

16

AMBER

I GROANED AS I WOKE UP IN BED, GREGORY'S ARM WAS DRAPED across me and it helped me relax. He was safe. My neck was a little stiff, but it didn't hurt to move. I cautiously sat up in bed, rubbing my temples, looking at my phone, and slowly turning my head to crack my neck. I had some missed texts...

Casey: Happy Wedding day girl! 🤍

Gemini: Good morning Mrs. Reynolds! 👰
Today is your day, so relax and text me if you need anything. The only words you should be worried about saying is "I Do." See you soon! 😄

Mimi Girlfriend: Got the new addy for today. You'll look beautiful, as you always do 😘😘

NEW ADDY? DID SOMETHING HAPPEN WITH THE VENUE? I SHOOK Gregory next to me. He jumped awake looking around the room starting to reached under the nightstand for the gun. Then relaxed when he saw me, laying back down. "Good morning, baby. How did you sleep? Are you sore?"

"No I feel fine for the most part. Mimi texted me that she received a new address. I still want to get married. Where is the wedding at?"

A small smile appeared on his lips. "Here, in about nine hours. The ceremony will still be at 6."

I froze. "Here like at our house? Oh fuck, we have to clean and and move the furniture. Where are people going to sit?" My heart started to race, I needed to hurry up and get ready so the bathrooms, kitchen and living room could be clean.

He placed his hand on my leg and slowly rubbed. "Baby, you aren't going to worry about anything today. I'm making sure of it, just make it to the altar. I got everything taken care of."

I chuckled. "You think I'd leave on our wedding day in our own house?"

He shrugged. "I'd hope not."

I kissed him and brushed my fingers through his beard. "I wouldn't and couldn't. I want Reynolds at the end of my name for at least the next sixty years or forever, whichever comes first."

He blushed and tried to hide his face. "I want to get as close to eternity as it takes." Then he looked me in the eye. "I want to wake up to your face every morning. Your beautiful face. The face of my wife."

"Isn't it bad luck to see me before the wedding?"

He shook his head and brushed my jaw, "There's no bad luck when true love is there. I wasn't taking a chance with not seeing your face as soon as I opened my eyes."

"Everyone will be here soon so I'll let you shower and everything. Mrs. Reynolds."

I stuck my tongue out. "I can't wait for you to say that the next time we fuck."

We chuckled and got out of bed. I can't have folks walk in while we're getting busy. Unless it was Gemini and Calvin, I can't wait to see Gemini naked. I went into the bathroom, then closed the door behind me, starting my routine.

I STEPPED OUT OF THE BATHROOM IN MY ROBE AND SAW CASEY typing on her phone and Gemini looking around the room at the different corners. They smiled as they looked at me. "Hey! I know you didn't pick us, but we are your honorary get-ready crew." Gemini said walking over and giving me a warm hug. If Casey wasn't here I'd squeeze her ass.

I chuckled. "Nobody was busting down the door to do that. When does make up get here?"

Casey looked up. "It's 10:00 a.m. now, hair and makeup will get here at two and we will need to be show ready by 5:30."

I looked around. "Think we have time to smoke? We can slide to the garage or backyard before it gets too crazy. Today is about relaxing, right?"

Gemini stood up. "Bet, I've got joints in my bag right now. We'll put on our robes and shit when we come back."

I looked at Casey as she held up a rolled backwood. "I brought four. I didn't know what kind of time we would be on."

We all laughed as we walked out of the bedroom. I headed into the kitchen to see my future husband washing dishes. He looked at us concerned. "We're about to smoke, want to come?"

He shook his head. "Nah I'm good. I'm locked in. Go on the back porch though."

The line we were walking in, turned and headed to the backyard. Denver was moving the couch as Calvin was vacuuming. Gemini blew a kiss at Calvin, that he caught like a football and placed on his lips. Casey gave Denver the middle finger and he laughed then winked at her. *So corny.*

We were two blunts in staring at the brick wall when Greg came out with wings and fries for all of us. "This is too greasy to eat RIGHT before I get in this dress," I complained.

"Smell it."

I inhaled the plate, sighed and began eating. "Okay I guess I can eat a little bit."

"Mmmhm."

After eating and taking an undisturbed nap, it was time to start getting ready. I wasn't allowed downstairs now. I wanted to be surprised anyway. I woke up to the makeup artist finishing Gemini's face. Now it was my turn.

I LOOKED IN THE MIRROR THE MAKEUP ARTIST HELD TO MY FACE. Our colors were burnt orange and dark earthy green that she used in my highlight. The winged eyeliner really highlighted my face shape and added some extra drama. The dress fit better than it did in the fitting room.

When everything was done, a light knock came at the door and Gemini peaked her head out. Was Gregory already trying to peek at me?

"You know a Mimi and Merlot?" she asked.

I gave a cheesy grin. "Yea you can let them in, they're my girlfriends."

Gem stepped to the side and let them in as they gasped looking at me. She hugged me before leaving the room.

Mimi's hand was on her lips. "Oh gosh Merlot. She looks beautiful. You remember when we got married?" Her eyes started to fill with tears.

Merlot gently touched her hand. "Baby you already cried on the way here."

"Yes, because it's intimate and so beautiful. I wish we got married at our house."

I rolled my eyes and opened my arms for them. As we hugged and rocked side to side, I felt even more at peace. They were my partners, even if they were married to each other. "You know," Merlot started. "This won't change anything with us unless you want it to."

I smiled and brushed my hand on her suit. "It shouldn't but I'll always let you both know."

Gemini awwed in the corner. "That's so beautiful."

They kissed my cheek and wished me luck as they all left the room.

Now it was just me. No neck pain, just excitement turning in my stomach. I'm about to get married. Fuck. I'm marrying the man of my dreams, and our partners are here to witness. In our house.

Wow.

I came down the stairs with my bouquet, I heard clicks from the photographer and smiled. I didn't know it could be this easy. I thought I'd have to run around with curlers hanging out of my hair like every movie with a wedding. But today has been carefree. I hope it's been the same experience for bae.

Then I heard my song, *"Until,"* playing loud throughout the house. As the song began, I hid behind the corner until the harmony of voices came in, giving me goosebumps. When I heard this song for the first time on the radio, I knew it was the song I'd walk down the aisle to.

I turned the corner, I was so nervous that I looked down as I walked onto the white petals and white rug. As I saw the bottom of the chairs, I slowly lifted my head up trying to focus. The living room felt completely different. Auburn curtains were on the side, complementing our pale furniture, emerald green ribbons were wrapped behind the chairs. I thought I would lose the rhythm of the song from the *awws*.

Step together. Step together.

Ms. Grant was smiling, Casey was holding up her phone, and Gemini was holding Calvin's hand. Then I glanced to the left and saw Mimi's cornrows and Merlot in a black suit smiling, they were holding hands as well. I turned my head toward the middle to see Gregory's face.

His auburn suit was perfect with a white button-down and white rose tucked into the jacket pocket. His lips were trembling. He tried to hide his face, but it wasn't working. He was crying, actually crying as he saw me. When I made it to him, I wiped the tear from my eye as Gemini reached up for my bouquet. I could barely listen to anything said before the vows. There were so many words in Gregory's eyes as he looked at me, adoration, grace, awe... love.

"The couple has chosen to write their own vows, Mr. Reynolds."

He took out the folded paper from his suit jacket, then mockingly cleared his throat. He already cried once, but I think he will again.

"Amber Cress, I have waited for this day since the first time I saw you. From that day until now, you've had a golden aura surrounding you. Cress, from the Greek history of Cressida, means golden and that's what you are to my life. Gold. Priceless, alluring, captivating. I promise to always provide and protect you with every fiber of my being. There is not a day that passes where you don't cross my mind. I want today with you, to forever. You're the woman I want to grow old with, no matter what. I will always protect you first. You have always been my top priority. My golden wife."

Now my lips were trembling.

"Amber, my love, my wife. I pray I have forever to show you how many different ways I love you as your husband. Your my guiding light, in sickness and in health, till death do us part."

Now I was full on crying. I always knew he felt like this, but hearing him say it and claim it made my heart explode. His bottom lip was quivering and he turned away as the minister handed both of us a tissue.

Now it was my turn.

Gemini handed me my phone as I mouthed, thank you. "Gregory Reynolds, when I met you, it was at a hard time in my life. One of the hardest times, actually. You didn't judge, just struck up a conversation that wasn't sexual or off-putting like what I was used to. You actually listened to what I had to say. You listened to me vent about both of my jobs, you always sent white roses on my hardest days, you take necessary time off so we can still have quality time together. You've shown me what true love feels like. Thank you for allowing me to rest on you."

I reached out and held his hand while my phone held the other, trembling.

"You have been patient and understanding in ways I will never understand. I love you with all my heart. I used to be scared of what forever would look like at our dynamic."

I glanced to Mimi and Merlot and they winked.

"You even understand that too. I promise to take care of you and give you what you need and remind you to take time for yourself. As your wife, I'll be the partner that looks out for you and has your back. I'll love you until the line of death separates us. Thanks for waiting for me to pick a date."

He rolled his eyes as the room chuckled, then he squeezed my hand and I squeezed it back, handing Gemini my phone back as she patted a tissue on her face. We placed our rings on each other's fingers and, DAMN the rock was big as fuck. He smiled wide when he saw the shock on my face.

The minister continued, "If anyone has any reason why these two should not wed, speak now or forever hold your peace."

Gregory and I both looked around the room with a "try me if you want to expression." Nobody said a peep.

"I now pronounce you, husband and wife. You may now kiss the bride."

Gregory bent down and kissed me. I was prepared for a peck. But we full on made out, his hand going up my back and all. There were a few coughs and I pulled back with a laugh.

"Now presenting, Gregory and Amber Reynolds!"

Everyone stood up and cheered us on as we walked back down the aisle.

"The couple will now enjoy their first dance, please step outside."

We did it. *We made it.*

17

GREG

I HELD AMBER'S HAND, GUIDED HER TO THE BACKYARD. WE DID it. A tent was up so everyone came in behind us, *Sweet Lady* by Tyreese was playing on the speakers as we made our way to the middle. I focused on her face and the smile growing even more on her face. The only other time I felt this light on my feet was on a football field after a touchdown.

When we finished we went to our table with a burgundy Mr. & Mrs. sitting in front of our seats. Amber shimmied when she saw them. It was really the little pieces that were making today more special.

I didn't notice the mic that was set up until Monte's voice boomed, "Is this on?"

The wedding planner held a thumbs up in the back. The tent wasn't huge but big enough for everyone to spread out. There were men in black suits at all entrances and at the end of the driveway. Nobody was getting through.

"Nah I have known Gregory since before he bought my old shop. He's seen a lot of thangs and impacted a lot of people. I've watched him mentor young boys and girls to show them how to make good decisions and how working on ole rinky dink cars can make you some money. It's not easy being everywhere at once, speaking at schools, running businesses. That's a lot on the shoulders of a Black man. But Mrs. Reynolds, if I can tell you anything, it's that he's a hardworking man that cares about you."

He looked directly at me. "Now Son, marriage is one of those thangs you have to keep working at to make it better. I've been married thirty-five years and still learnin' about my wife. But as long as yall keep God first, a Bible handy and a shotgun close by, you will be alright."

The room burst into laughs, including Amber and me as we stood up, giving him a dap then a hug.

"And listen tuh your wife. Every time I don't listen, I'm in trouble. God gives women a discerning spirit for a reason."

"Yes sir," I said, shaking his hand.

It seemed like almost everyone spoke on the mic and had words of advice or stories to share. When Gemini and Calvin were walking up together hand in hand, I actually felt nervous. Amber gently rubbed my hand in reassurance.

Calvin spoke first. "If you went to school with us, you know when you saw Greg, you saw me or the other way around. Except on the football field cause yall know I'm not that athletic." People chuckled as Coraline yelled, "true." He eyed her and kept going. "We have brought the best and worst out of each other. I'm glad to have Amber in our fold of friendship." He held up his glass toward us. "To the Reynolds."

Gemini raised her glass next to Calvin and smiled even more.

Then we danced. Well, everyone else danced as I two stepped until Amber forced me to do the *Cupid Shuffle*. Today felt so good. I had a small ache in my back but I could ignore it. I can go get a massage next week.

Today has been worth the wait.

After a few hours, people started filing out. I dapped security before they left and thanked them for everything. Then we went back inside our home.

The Reynolds's home.

"So what were you doing before everything? Besides the dishes," Amber asked me with a chuckle.

"Mainly helping set up. When Calvin and Denver made it, we did the heavy lifting so the set up and break down would be easier and quicker. Then, we took some shots and smoked before getting ready. After that," he kissed my hand. "You became my wife."

"I didn't see Ayden out there. He couldn't make it?"

I shook my head. "No he hasn't been telling people when he's home since all that crazy shit happened the last time."

She hummed. "I forgot. Well, I hope he doesn't blame himself. He did send 'The Bull' after them."

I shook my head. "Bull helped me more than a few times growing up. But I still wish I didn't ask to help serve as a kid, you know. That got Ayden and me in trouble, A even took all the heat and did the time."

"If you could, would you have invited Bull?"

She gave me the inquisitive look where I knew I couldn't lie to her. "I would have. He was a dick, but I still miss him. I bet he would've tried Ms. Grant still."

Amber laughed and I joined in. "She looked great in that dress. You know what they say, baby daddies don't stop loving baby mamas."

I shook my head. "Well I refused for someone to call you my baby mama, this is my wife right here. How's your head and neck feeling?"

"Pretty good. I might have a heating pad close to the bed just in case I need to pop it and have it in bed. But right now, even after dancing and everything, I'm feeling okay."

I gently grabbed her chin and pulled her into a kiss.

Everything was worth the wait.

Now I can't wait for what the future may bring.

TWO WEEKS LATER: GREG

I'm a married man!

I've never been happier nigga, no cap. I smile every time I look at the ring Amber put on my finger. Yea, that's my wife and future mother of my kids. I wouldn't change anything, everything happens for a reason. I've still been low-key. I did a big reup from a resource in LA so I've been moving around more, just only repeat clients that know the deal. I need as much bread as I can get for this resort. We leave for our honeymoon in two weeks. Amber has been officially cleared by her doctor.

Did she want to rest? Hell nah.

She listed the two units that are move in ready and we had good applicants in less than a week. She background checked the tenants while the leases were finalized by a lawyer. I read them over myself and they were perfect. The next thing I know, our first tenants had set in stone move in dates. How she's able to move so fast always amazes me. She deserves this honeymoon too. We need a real break after everything that happened leading up to our wedding.

I was having one of those rare moments where I was home

alone. No orders. No demands. Amber on a date, so it's just me and my mind at the dead of night.

My other phone rang, only Coraline and close drug affiliates had it. I checked the caller ID and saw Big C. *Coraline.* I answered it, trying to sound calm. I could feel that something was wrong. "Yo?"

"Aye Greg," a chill went down my spine. It was D. I can't forget his visit to the library when I wasn't there. "You've been real low key. Aint nobody seen you for real, so I had to call you myself. I want you, nigga. That's why I had to call you from your friends phone. I already paid a visit to your other crib, but you weren't there either. Check your phone."

Just then, a photo *dinged* on my wallpaper from an unsaved 678 phone number. It was a picture of the street library Amber and I made together, but broken into pieces across the sidewalk. The art, the books, destroyed. That means he knows where Amber is too *and* our property. She's been there so many times without protection. What if he did more? What if he started threatening the people moving in.

I brought the phone back to my ear, sounding unbothered and even toned. "So you only got Coraline?"

He chuckled nastily in my ear. "Yea, your big rich friend, Coraline Grant. So if I got her phone, then you already know I got her. I haven't hurt her...yet. She's pretty to look at though."

"I'm a Queen pin! I can't wait to fuck you up!" I heard yelled in the background. That was her voice, so she was still alive.

"Shut up bitch! Aye man, you better pull up to the cigar lounge in less than thirty or I'll start cutting her toes off. Your timer starts now nigga."

Call ended.

Fuck.

The End

ACKNOWLEDGEMENT

Yall it's book three of the series can you believe it!

I'm so glad that you read Greg and Amber's story, while getting an update on what the Grant family is up to. I'm so proud of not only them, but you the reader for reading this!

I want to thank God for the ability to share these stories. I also want to thank my daughter for being amazing and growing into herself! I want to thank my husband for supporting me and encouraging my dreams. Also big shout out to my family and friends!

This isn't the end of The Book at the Bar series. I truly enjoy this world that came from my debut novel, The Book at the Bar.

Don't forget to leave your **review on Amazon , Goodreads and/or StoryGraph!** Every review helps support indie authors like me!

Love you!

ABOUT THE AUTHOR

Kirahvi is a Florida born and Georgia living author that loves love. Throughout her childhood, Kirahvi spent her free time writing heartfelt poems and short stories in fictional lands. After graduating with an MBA, she fell deeper in love with the romance genre.

She enjoys the beach as much as a cabin in the mountains. When not recording for social media, she's at a library, park or listening to a vinyl record. She is married to her high school sweetheart and the family waves their Buccaneers flag high!

Follow her on Instagram, TikTok, YouTube, Threads and Facebook on @Kirahvi_ReadsnWrites or visit her website www. kirahvibello.com for more information about her and events coming soon.

Don't forget to leave your **review on Amazon , Goodreads and/or StoryGraph!** Every review helps support indie authors like me!